THE CAT THAT WAS LEFT BEHIND

The cat padded out of the underbrush and kept coming straight toward Chad, his pupils trusting black seeds in the centers of his yellow eyes. He plunked himself down in Chad's lap, and Chad stroked him from head to tail, then scratched around his ears. A ragged purr began in the cat's throat.

"Hey cat, my cat," Chad whispered.

Chad is spending the summer on Cape Cod with the Sorenics, his foster family. They do their best to make him feel comfortable, but Chad ignores all offers of friendship. His real mother has rejected him, and he feels lost and terribly alone—until he finds the stray cat that seems even more rootless and unloved than he.

In a novel full of the sights and smells of a summer by the ocean, C.S. Adler tells the moving story of a boy's groping for affection, and a cat's reluctance to trust him.

THE CAT THAT
WAS LEFT BEHIND

The Cat That Was Left Behind

by

C. S. Adler

Clarion Books

TICKNOR & FIELDS : A HOUGHTON MIFFLIN COMPANY
New York

Clarion Books
Ticknor & Fields, a Houghton Mifflin Company
Copyright © 1981 by C.S. Adler.

Library of Congress Cataloging in Publication Data
Adler, C.S.   The cat that was left behind.
SUMMARY: Chad doesn't think his new foster family
will be any better than the others, but after getting
to know them during a summer at the Cape and after
meeting a stray cat, he begins to change his mind.
[1.   Foster home care—Fiction.   2. Cats—Fiction]   I. Title.
PZ7.A26145Cat   [Fic]   80-28123
ISBN 0-395-31020-2

Cover art by Troy Howell

s 10 9 8 7 6 5 4 3 2

For Clifford, our son,
who lives with a flourish and
makes life exciting.

Chapter 1

Chad's thin thirteen-year-old body merged into the trunk of the big pitch pine on the hill behind the cottage. He stood perfectly still waiting for the cat. For two mornings in a row he had seen the cat pause here to stare down at the cottage before vanishing into the scrub oak and bearberry. The cat didn't look like anybody's pet. It looked like a wild creature, beholden to nobody, strong—the way Chad wanted to be.

Looking down at the cottage Chad could see his foster family stuffing the back of their asthmatic old station wagon with baskets and colorful beach towels, a red-and-blue-striped rubber raft, blankets to spread on the sand. After the mother, followed by her big redheaded daughter and husky son, got into the car, the father called, "Change your mind yet, Chad?"

"No," Chad answered.

"You ought to give it another try. The ocean's going to be great today." The coaxing sounded phony coming from the short, muscular father who was more used to issuing commands.

"I'll be okay here," Chad yelled back, and held his breath hoping they would let him be. He only relaxed when the car left. It felt good to be alone. In every foster family where he had ever lived, a jumble of kids surrounded him. His private space rarely reached beyond his own skin. Now he could wait for the cat without having to defend himself against anyone, or watch out for anyone, or obey anyone. He could think his own thoughts in peace for a change. More than anything, Chad hated this living with strangers, people he didn't care about—or if he learned to care about them, people who disappeared from his life soon after.

He inhaled the piney scent of the woods. The trees were strange, dwarfed, twisty things that scrabbled for a hold in the sand and hunched low out of the salt wind.

"Lots of poison ivy about," the father had warned. "Do you know how to recognize it?"

"Everybody knows that," Chad had said.

"Blueberries all over the hill too," the mother had added cheerfully, trying to capture Chad with her smile.

Chad had never seen blueberries growing wild,

never seen the ocean before either. He didn't like it, didn't like the way the waves crashed down, rushing at him like monsters out to get him.

"It isn't always this rough," she had said—the mother. Pam was her name.

What was he supposed to call her? The ones he hated most said to call them "Mother." Those who had kept foster children before at least knew enough to tell him what to call them at the start. These people had never taken in a foster kid before. He *would* have the bad luck to be first. And when he'd asked his caseworker what the Sorenics needed him for if they already had two kids of their own, she'd gone on about how their minister had inspired them to want to share their blessings with those less fortunate.

That made Chad sick, like he was a charity case. Who were they kidding anyway? He knew the county paid for his keep. Probably the Sorenics needed the money. Well, that's all they'd get out of keeping him this summer. He wasn't going to be "company," as the mother had suggested, for either their shy, freckle-faced daughter or their big, shut-mouthed lump of a son. Chad was done with pleasing people. So what if they didn't like him. All they could do was throw him back to his caseworker after the summer, and they'd do that anyway whether or not he turned himself inside out for them.

The cat appeared like a small black-silk genie. A white exclamation mark covered one half of its face. Its feet and chest were white too. When it saw Chad, black marbles of fear eclipsed the surrounding amber of its eyes. Chad kept still, hoping not to scare the cat away. It looked young, but one ear had been notched, in a fight probably, and it was hungry-lean.

Cautiously, with eyes fixed on the boy, the cat eased itself back into the undergrowth and was gone. Chad was disappointed. So long a wait for so short a meeting! He would have to tempt the cat with something more than his company next time—food maybe. Tomorrow he would set some food out, tomorrow when the cat came again.

Chad ambled back into the cottage, pleased to have it to himself. The rooms were small and pleasantly shabby—faded upholstery couch and chairs, floors already scuffed and sandy though they had all pitched in to help the mother, Pam, clean the place up when they arrived two days ago. Pam was a smiler with dark, shiny eyes, but she was not as pretty as his own mother; she was too skinny and dark. Chad's mother was pearly skinned and soft with light brown hair and dreaming blue eyes.

"I'll take you away with me next time I come," his mother always told him. Everytime she visited him, wherever he was living, she had promised, "Next time I'll take you with me." Everytime she said it, he believed her. "I love you so much, Chad Thomas," she would say. A dozen times since he was five she had told him how much she loved him. She did love him, he knew, but she had never taken him with her. Once she had bought him a toy sailboat and another time a baseball cap. She had given him a prayer book and a cowboy shirt with pearl buttons, but she never took him with her, and now she had written that letter.

Chad walked into the bedroom he shared with the boy, Bob Sorenic, and took the letter out of the duffle bag which held everything he owned. Patiently, he searched the letter for the third time, not sure what he was looking for unless it was a clue that she did not really mean it.

... I do not want you ever to think that I don't love you Chad. Your my baby boy and you will always be in my heart but this is my one chance now. This is a good man whose asked me to marry him and will marry me in a church and we will have children together and he will give them his name. You can't understand probably what that means to me but it means alot Chad and I'm sorry I couldn't raise you proper the way a mother should but I done what I could. And if I could of took you with me now I would of but this man says he don't want to take you to raise because I wasn't married proper in a church when I had you. He has powerful feelings about religion which I am coming to too and I hope you will someday. Anyways, the caseworker says that people who take children to adopt have to really love them just like they're own. I know your going to find fine people to adopt you because your such a good boy. God bless you always. Your loving mother,

April Anne.

Lightly Chad traced the sharp creases of the much-folded note paper with his finger. "I love you, but I can't have you with me," she said. The man didn't want him. Maybe she would decide not to marry the man after all. Maybe she would leave the man in the church and come after Chad and say, "You are my only son, Chad, and I love you most."

Then he would say, "Don't worry, Mama. I'll take care of you. Now I'm thirteen, and that's old enough."

Soon he could get a job, maybe even now if he lied about his age. Except he had a little kid's face and he was not all that tall. But he could probably get some kind of work, and then she would not need a man to marry her in a church and take care of her and give her other children.

Chad wondered for the hundredth time how come that man who had been his father had not married his mother long ago when he was born. Even though Chad had never known him, he hated that man. He hated them all, except his mother. "April Anne, April Anne, Mama!" he crooned to himself and muffled his longing in the pillow on the bottom bunk bed that belonged to Bob Sorenic.

Chapter 2

When Chad heard the car pull up he ducked into the bathroom to wash the feelings off his face. His face never did hide his feelings right.

"You should have come with us, Chad. The water was great," Mr. Sorenic said when Chad came out of the bathroom. "Bob and I swam at least—what do you say, Bob?—a mile?"

"No way, Dad!" Bob was only twelve, but bigger and broader and probably stronger than Chad; dark like his mother and athletic-looking like his father. Jocks! Chad hated jocks. They always acted like they were such hotshots and pushed people around.

"Polly, I think you got too much sun. You're all pink. Where did we put the skin cream?" Pam asked and went into the bathroom to find it.

Polly was built solid like her father and her brother, but she had a gentle look and gobs of curly red hair. All she ever did was read.

"The beach was lovely today, all sparkly and warm," Pam said to Chad when she returned with the blue jar of cream. "Polly and I found some sea clams. We're going to try cooking them as an appetizer for lunch. What did you do while we were gone, Chad?"

"Nothing. Just hung around."

"Weren't you bored all alone doing nothing?"

"No. I like being alone."

"Dad," Bob asked, "did you reserve that old tennis court by the pier like you said?"

"You bet," Mr. Sorenic replied. "I brought a racket along for you to use, Chad. Do you know how to play?"

"No."

"Well, that's no problem. I'll teach you. I'm the tennis coach at our high school. You know that I'm a physical education teacher, don't you? You'll get private instructions free for nothing."

"No, thanks."

"How come?" Mr. Sorenic sounded surprised.

"I don't want to learn tennis."

"How do you know until you try it? It's a great game, a life sport. You're got to *try* it at least."

"I don't—" Chad began but shut up. It was not smart to fight too hard. Even though the caseworker had only dumped him on this family a couple of days ago, the same day they drove up here, they could still ship him right back if he was too difficult. Then he'd probably get stuck in the Children's Shelter, where they had more rules and restrictions than any house he'd ever lived in. It was like being in cold storage, that shelter, like jail probably was. "Okay," Chad said. "I'll try it."

Mr. Sorenic cheered up right away. Then Pam announced lunch. She and Polly served the sea clams which tasted like flat rubber balls to Chad. Everybody made sandwiches for themselves from the plates of cold cuts and cheese on the table. The table was set with real dishes, not paper ones.

"How come you don't use paper plates?" Chad asked.

"What for?" Pam wanted to know.

"Then nobody has to do the dishes."

"But real plates are nicer and more economical besides," Pam said. "I think they're worth the extra trouble."

Why not, Chad thought. She could make the kids do the dishes anyway. Sure enough that was what happened. "I'll take my turn now," Polly said. "Then you guys can go play tennis."

"Fair enough," her father agreed. He sounded like a big kid eager to get outside to play.

Chad trailed behind Bob and his father who jogged down the macadam road that ran past the piney hill where the summer cottage sat. The cottage was close to the harbor, a mile from the Wellfleet marina past the harbor beaches lined with cramped rental cottages and motels. Passing cars nearly skinned them on the narrow road, but Mr. Sorenic and Bob did not seem to worry about it. Chad half walked, half ran after them.

The tennis courts were right next to the marina parking lot behind a bait-and-tackle shop and a soft-ice cream stand. "Boy, are these in rotten shape!" Bob complained, looking at the cracks and heaves in the surface of the courts and the holes in the wire link fence.

"You want to dig into your savings, Bob? You can pay for the courts at the yacht club."

"There isn't even a backboard here."

"Use the side of the building over there in the parking lot. Look, it's not the condition of the courts that's going to make you good; it's how much practicing you're willing to put in. Like I told you, you can win the junior tournament this fall if you set your mind to it."

"I hear you. Okay, whatever you say," Bob said. His fleshy face tightened in readiness.

"Chad, how about just watching us for a few minutes while we warm up?"

Chad slumped at the corner of the net, fiddling with the crank that was supposed to raise and lower it but which was too rusted to work. He heard the thwack of the balls rocketing back and forth and saw the long, hard swings the players were taking. It looked too serious to be a game. *What's he got me here for?* Chad wondered resentfully. He looked over his shoulder at the dirty brown sand littered with rocks, sticks, shells, and seaweed, and licked by the greenish water. One of the toy-sized sails that tagged the flat expanse went over. Chad caught his breath, but in no time the person who had fallen off the boat popped the sail up out of the water and set off again as if nothing had happened. It didn't look dangerous the way the ocean side did. Were there any sharks in the harbor? Probably not with all those boats going in and out.

"What say you and I hit a few now?" Mr. Sorenic called.

"Me?" Chad came to with alarm. He had been lulled by the sun on the back of his neck and the pleasant sounds—cries of the gulls, swish of passing cars. Now he tensed up.

"It's okay," Chad said. "He can practice. I don't mind watching."

"Bob's going to hit a few off the building now. Do you know how to hold a racquet?"

"No."

Mr. Sorenic came up to the net and showed him. "You hold it like you're shaking hands with it."

Chad adjusted his hand nervously.

"That's fine. Now the main thing to remember when you hit is to keep the racquet parallel to the ground. Your returns should be low and hard eventually when you get the hang of it. Just remember for now to keep the racquet parallel to the ground and get your arm back when you start the swing."

Chad swallowed and began to perspire. He wanted to have it done with and be heading back to the cottage. Mr. Sorenic began hand tossing him soft balls. Chad swung wildly at each one, missing more often than not, sending balls wide and high to left and right when he did manage to get the racquet on them.

"What are you so tense about?" Mr. Sorenic asked. "Relax. Nobody's keeping score."

"I'm not good at ball games," Chad mumbled.

"You'll do okay . . . Just take it easy. Everybody should learn to play tennis."

The racquet swished uselessly through the air. When would this guy let up on him? Bob was hitting balls off the side of the building in a steady rhythm. Chad could hear the solid thwack, thwack, thwack. Bob's father kept standing there on the other side of the net calmly tossing balls at Chad.

"Your timing's off because you're trying too hard. Relax," he kept saying.

Chad got mad. Why do I have to do this, he wanted to yell. Are you some kind of weirdo who likes to see a guy suffer? Perspiration was trickling down his back and chest and face when the man finally said, "Okay, let's call it a day. You'll do all right, Chad, as soon as you relax. We have all summer after all. Do you want to watch while Bob and I work on his backhand for a while?"

"No. I'll head back now."

"Okay, you jog on home and tell the girls we're on our way."

His sudden release gave Chad a spurt of energy. He began jogging back to the cottage, feeling relief with every bit of distance he put between himself and the courts. Halfway back he realized he didn't have to run if he didn't want to. He stopped and began to shamble along, looking around him.

Suddenly he glimpsed a cat sniffing at the dried seaweed on the beach. Was that his cat? He crossed the road and walked between a big brown boathouse and a private home with a huge screened porch. The cat drifted on, heading toward the marina. It was small and black. Its long tail twitched while its thin body shadowed the sand. It stopped to sniff at something and Chad saw the white under the black head. Of course, lots of black-and-white cats could live around here. Chad took long strides in the sand back toward the marina after the cat, trying to catch up with it. The cat saw him. Immediately it streaked off. It *was* his cat. Chad had seen the white exclamation mark on its face. Chad sat down on the sand to rest a while and study the boats in the harbor.

"Where were you?" Mr. Sorenic asked when Chad got back to find father and son already at the cottage.

"Just looking around."

"You can't just take off without letting us know where you're going, Chad. That's a family rule around here."

"I didn't take off," Chad said sullenly.

"Not good enough," Mr. Sorenic insisted. "It shouldn't have taken you an hour to cover a mile. I'm not trying to hassle you, Chad, but you need to get the rules straight right from the start. We operate as a unit around here—all for all. We cooperate with each other, and that means not keeping other people back from doing what they want because they don't know where you are and have to wait up for you."

"Okay," Chad said, "okay!" He thought the lecture was way too heavy for this one little tardiness.

"Good heavens, Roger," Pam said soothingly, "Chad was only a little delayed."

"I'm not punishing him, Pam, just communicating how we behave around here."

The two adults stood there saying things at each other with their eyes. Chad butted in abruptly,

"What's the rule on what to call you?" He figured so long as he was in the hornet's nest already, he might as well risk a few more stings.

"No rule on that," Mr. Sorenic said, "though I think . . ."

"What do *you* think, Chad?" Pam interrupted her husband. "What would you be comfortable with?"

"I could call you by your names, Pam and —" he hesitated. "Roger." He forced himself to say it though this was not a man Chad felt comfortable calling by his first name.

"A little casual for me," Roger said mildly.

"Mr. and Mrs. Sorenic then," Chad countered fast. He was not going to call this thick-skinned, hard-nosed guy *Father*.

"Fine," Roger said. "Is that okay with you, Pam?"

"It's so formal," Pam said. "What's wrong with being casual? Cape Cod's a casual place, and Chad's not a stranger. He's part of the family."

Roger tried to cow her with his frown but she didn't back down. Chad wondered if Roger would give it to her later for interfering, but she didn't look worried. All Roger said to her was, "Okay, boss, have it your way." Then, as if he couldn't care less about the whole discussion, Roger stretched and shook his powerful shoulder muscles. "Well, now," he said, "let's get the show on the road here. Are we going back to the ocean or do you guys feel like checking out the bay beach?"

"Polly got enough sun for one day. Don't you think so?"

"I can cover up, Mom. I'd love to go for a walk on the bay beach."

Polly closed the book on her finger to hold the place. Chad had not yet seen her without a book in her hand.

They all got in the car, with Bob and Chad squeezing Polly in on either side in the back seat. Everyone had gotten ready to take off for the beach too fast for Chad to invent a good excuse not to go. Now that he was committed, he hunkered down in the seat preparing to endure it.

"So, Chad, think you're going to like tennis?" Roger asked over his shoulder as he drove.

"I hate it," Chad said.

"You don't like much, do you?" Bob said with a smirk.

"Whatdaya mean?"

"Well, that's what you said about the ocean and about the sea clams."

Chad squeezed the fingers of one hand as hard as he could with the other, then reversed and squeezed again, lifting his face to the cool wind coming through the car window. He ignored Bob and all the rest of them too. Who cares what they think of me, he told himself, just so long as they leave me alone.

When they parked at the bay beach parking lot, he thought at first the bay was just like the ocean except the distance from the parking lot to the water was shorter and the dunes were smaller. Then he saw the major difference with relief. This was calm water, like the harbor only cleaner-looking, sparkling and flat like a lake he had been to with one foster family years ago. He could take this all right. Only he didn't like having to stick by the Sorenics. All their attention to him made Chad feel like a dog on a leash.

Reluctantly he sat down on the sand next to the blanket Pam and Polly had spread out and anchored with bags and snorkeling gear. Roger and Bob immediately started flipping a Frisbee at each other. Chad could handle a Frisbee all right, but he was not about to say so. He hunched down with his arms around his legs and stared at the sand. A translucent, sand-colored creature as big as a large bug rose from a quarter-size hole and scuttled off sideways.

"Hey," Chad said. "Is that a crab?" As soon as he'd blurted out the question, he felt exposed. Questions gave people an excuse to laugh at your ignorance, Chad had learned. But nobody laughed.

"That's a sand crab," Pam said. "Lots around but they don't bother anything . . . Chad, are you afraid of getting too much sun?"

"What?" He looked at the woman lying there with that eager, let's-like-each-other smile on her face and looked away. She reminded him of a first-grade teacher he had once cared about. The caseworker had told him Mrs. Sorenic was a school nurse. That figured. Same type.

"You still have your jacket on," Pam said.

"Oh, yeah." He shucked off the jacket. His olive skin tanned easily.

"I'm going to take a walk up the beach toward the point, Mother," Polly said.

"Go ahead, honey," Pam answered, opening the book she had in her hand. Chad wondered what they'd think if he admitted he had never finished a whole book in his life. That he was a moron probably.

Polly stood up and hesitated. She was looking at him. Chad looked back. "Would you like to come for a walk with me?" Her voice was high and thin with shyness.

"Sure," Chad answered at once before she could be sorry she had risked asking and before he even decided if he wanted to go with her or not.

Polly left a trail of footprints in the sand ahead of him. Chad amused himself by fitting his steps into hers. Polly was all covered up in a long-sleeved blouse and jeans and a floppy cotton hat. Every once in a while she bent and picked up a shell or a twist of driftwood from the matted straw stuff that smelled of fish and salt. Before long they were out of sight of the people sitting on the beach. All Chad could see was Polly and the water and the beach until it was swallowed up by sky.

"I guess if you like to be alone, this is the place to go all right," Chad said, looking across the rippled water at the gray rim of the horizon. Not even a boat was visible.

Polly stopped and looked back at him. "You said you liked to be alone."

"Yeah, but a place like this—you sure couldn't survive here unless you had a camp trailer or something full up with food."

"I don't understand what you mean." She dropped back to walk beside Chad.

"It's a thing I do," he said. "Wherever I am, I figure out if I could live there—like in the woods, there's berries and water and little animals you could trap, and like in a city, there's always ways to get food in a city—use garbage cans if you have to, but here . . ."

"You could fish," Polly said. "There's clams when the tide goes out, and you can catch flounder and bluefish and bass off the shore. You can eat some kinds of seaweed, and for water, well, you could always go to somebody's house and ask for water, couldn't you?"

"It wouldn't be easy here though," he said.

"Not very comfortable either."

"I don't care about being comfortable," Chad boasted.

"I do," she said.

Chad kicked at the black stringy stuff mixed with the blond straw which formed two irregular bands along the beach above the stony edge of the water. "What's this stuff called anyway?"

"That's *wrack*. You've never been to the beach before?"

"No." He checked her face to see if she was going to put him down for that, but her expression hadn't changed. "How come you read so much?" Chad asked her.

Polly looked away so that her coppery hair hid her face and said vaguely, "I don't know."

"I mean," he persisted, "you're always reading. You gotta be finding something in it."

"I guess I'm curious about other people's lives."

"That's what you're reading books for? If you want to learn about people, what you ought to do is talk to people, real people, not ones in books."

"I think people in books are more real than real people," Polly said. "At least to me they are because, well, like in a book you know what somebody's thinking. You find out all about a person, not just the little bits they tell you. And you don't have to wait months to find out what's going to happen to them. You just read the next chapter."

"But they're just make-believe, the people in books."

"Not to me."

21

Chad thought about it. It was true most people didn't tell you what they were thinking, but you could watch them closely and pretty well figure it out—sometimes. As to finding out what was going to happen, well, Polly had a point there. He could see it might be nice not to have to wait. Waiting was a drag. Like now he was waiting until he could figure out what to do about his mother. And he was going to have to wait forever until he turned eighteen and could be rid of all the meddling strangers in his life. When he was eighteen, he would be on his own! Freedom!

"Look," Polly said, pointing at half a dozen small brownish birds on extra long, pick-up-stick legs twiddling along the water's edge. "I love sandpipers."

"They're funny," Chad said.

"I'd rather walk on a beach than anywhere in the world," Polly said with a passion that made Chad think she was funny too.

"What grade are you in?" he asked, trying to guess her age. She was big-boned, taller than he, but she had not rounded out yet the way teenaged girls did.

"I'm in tenth, a sophomore." She glanced at him. "I skipped a grade because of my reading. I'm fourteen and should be in ninth really."

Chad had been proud of being in eighth grade which was where he was supposed to be. Most foster kids he knew were years behind because of the missed schooling. They sat around in temporary homes or at the Children's Shelter not going to school, just sitting and waiting for the next foster home placement or for whatever the court would decide to do with them. But whenever he got into a class, he had been able to catch on fast to what was going on. Even though he hated to read, he learned a lot just by listening.

"I've got a good memory," Chad said out of the middle of his own thoughts.

"I'll bet you do," she answered. "I'll bet you're smart."

"There's all kinds of ways of being smart. And most of them don't have to do with school."

Polly nodded, accepting his judgment. An all-right girl, Chad decided, nice really.

They walked to where the jeep tracks of fishermen made a crisscross of furrows in the soft sand that stretched out to where the broad bay blended into the neck of the harbor. Chad was tired, but he waited until Polly suggested, "Maybe we ought to turn around. They might want to start back for the cottage."

"Okay," he agreed casually.

"How was your walk?" Pam asked, smiling at them when Polly dropped onto the blanket on one side of her and Chad sat down on the sand on the other.

"Good," Chad said.

"Nice," Polly said. She picked up her book and opened it to where she had left a piece of straw as a marker.

Roger and Bob were horsing around in the water. Chad considered going in. He could swim all right. He had learned when he was eight at the YMCA pool, but the water here was colder than he was used to and he didn't know how soon it got deep. It wouldn't be smart to mix with those two guys anyway. He crossed his arms behind his head to make a pillow and lay back, closing his eyes against the sun which seemed to be aiming right at his eyeballs. A big green fly buzzed and settled on his leg. He smacked it dead and settled back.

He hadn't slept much last night or the night before. He never did sleep well in a new place. No way to defend himself while he was sleeping. Not that he'd ever been attacked the way one kid he knew had been, but he'd been ripped off a couple of times. His eyes closed. Then he was dreaming, the good dream about his mother, the one where she came to get him and took him away to live with her. This time she took him to a cottage on a beach. It was so real that he hated to wake up when Pam called his name. "Time to leave," she said. Soon, he promised himself, soon he'd make it be more than a dream.

Chapter 3

C had took his turn doing the breakfast dishes. He had saved half his glass of milk for the cat, and he was considering whether to snitch an egg or to ask Pam for one. If he asked, Pam would want to know what he needed an egg for, and then she would find out about the cat. He'd better stick to just the milk this morning.

"Chad," Roger said, "this morning we're going to repair the screens—you, Bob, and me."

"Do I have to help?"

Roger stiffened. Chad could feel him standing there behind him in the kitchen. Chad took a dish from the dishpan, rinsed it carefully and set it to drain. Finally Roger said, "Seems to me that seeing as you're part of this family now you ought to be willing to pitch in and help with family projects. I mean, just on general principles."

"I am pitching in." Chad took another dish up as evidence, but Roger ignored that.

He said, "Working is good for you. You get a sense of accomplishment from work. You know what I mean?"

"Yeah, I work. When people pay me."

Roger snorted angrily and walked out. For a minute Chad regretted having been so smart-mouthed. He felt enough in the wrong that he went outside to look for Roger when he had finished the dishes.

Roger was hammering a new screen door together to replace the one that opened into the living room. Bob was nearby, bending the prongs of patches to cover holes in a window screen. A big pile of screens waited to be patched. Chad watched them work, teetering on the edge of offering to help. They pretended he wasn't there. He almost told Bob, "I can do that," but he didn't want to give them a chance to tell him to get lost. He kicked a pinecone around for a while, and when they still ignored him, decided "To hell with them."

Nobody was left in the kitchen. He could hear Pam talking in Polly's bedroom. Quietly, he took a tinfoil dish and the half glass of milk he'd stowed in the refrigerator and slipped out the kitchen door. He set out the dish of milk a few feet from the pine tree on the hill. Then he waited. He was good at waiting. He could hold absolutely still and let his mind loose to figure out ways to handle whatever needed handling in his life. Figuring out people was what it came down to mostly. Figuring out how to act so as to stay out of trouble. Like now, he felt like taking off and going to Glens Falls in New York to find his mother so he could talk her into being with him instead of that man.

The thing was, there was no sense talking to her unless he got some kind of job first to show he could take care of her. She'd never be convinced he could take care of her otherwise. That was the real obstacle. Suppose he got picked up before he got a job! They would stick a PINS on him, a Person In Need of Supervision. Then he would end up in court and then either a boys' home or, if he were lucky, another foster family. No. He'd better not just take off like that.

Maybe he could write to his mother, tell her how he felt. It wouldn't work as well as seeing her, but for now it was probably the best he could do. He started composing his letter in his head. Nothing he thought of to say sounded tempting enough. His mother was never going to be won over by something that wasn't right there in front of her to touch. Maybe if he could send some money! That would say loud and clear, "See, I can take care of you."

The cat accepted his presence without surprise this time. It sat on its haunches watching him with a rim of amber showing around the black wariness in the center of its eyes.

"Hi, kitty," Chad whispered. "I brought you some milk."

As if it understood, the cat's eyes flicked to the tinfoil dish sitting on the pine needles halfway between them. Cautiously Chad lowered himself to a squat. "Come on, kitty. I'm not going to hurt you."

A red tongue, thin as an apple paring, licked out and withdrew leaving a trembling tip showing. The cat was hungry. Chad waited. "You're a good-looking kitty. I bet you're pretty young. You and me, we could be good friends. Come on and try the milk. It's okay."

He crouched, patiently waiting. Even so the cat started drawing back into the brush. Chad swallowed the tinny taste of disappointment. The cat was too wary. It would never be friends with him. Chad got up and headed back to the cottage. Halfway there he looked back and saw the cat lapping up the milk in comical haste.

He grinned, "Why you little sneak! You fooled me good." The cat raised its triangular head, watching him while it's red tongue flapped about like a dish towel, cleaning its face. "Okay," Chad said. "Two can play at that game." He stepped inside the cottage, watching the cat through the screen door to the kitchen.

"We're going to the ocean beach now, Chad. Do you have your swim trunks ready?" Roger asked.

"No, I'd rather stay here. If you don't mind."

"What's the matter? Do we have body odor or something?" Roger asked with heavy humor. "We're not such bad people when you get to know us."

"It's not—I mean, you're nice people," Chad began, then stopped and reminded himself: Never defend; you win by attack. "It's just I don't see why I can't stay here alone if I want. Why do I *have* to go to the beach?"

"You don't. But you might like it if you gave it a chance."

"See, I never get a chance to do the things I want. I've always gotta go along with what other people want."

"That's the condition most of us live with," Roger said drily.

"Roger!" Pam intervened for Chad again. "Chad's asking you for something that's not very hard to grant."

"When do I ever get to win one around here?" Roger asked the ceiling. "All right. Come on, you kids. We'll go to the beach and Chad can stay back and twiddle his toes or whatever he wants to do."

Pam grimaced as if her husband's reaction embarrassed her, but she just picked up an armload of towels and followed him out the front door.

As soon as they had driven away, Chad set off for the dirty harbor beach where he had seen the cat yesterday. He walked along the beach all the way past the tennis courts and onto the docks without seeing the cat once. A big pier with pilings, high and fat as telephone poles, jutted out over the water, forming a protective arm for the docked pleasure boats to nestle behind.

Chad strolled onto the pier. A father and two little kids were fishing on one side. Out at the end an old man, as ramshackle-looking as the Sorenics' cottage, was sitting on a box, fishing. Facing him a few feet away was the cat. Chad's spirits rose. He walked over to the old man. The cat didn't budge.

"Hi," Chad said. "Is that your cat?"

"That? No. I got no pets. That's just a stray."

"He must like you though."

"How do you figure that?" The old man peered at Chad through sharp blue eyes from behind a face full of grizzled whiskers.

"He won't come near me. I tried to make friends with him but he keeps his distance."

"Yeah, well, so would you if they left you behind when you was just a little kitten. He could of starved to death before he learned to fend for himself."

"Who left him?"

"Summer cottage renters. With people like that there's always a few strays after the summer. They feed the animals and think they're doing good, but then they don't want to take them when they go back home. So they just go off and leave them. Then the animals starve to death or get killed. This one survived. He's a smart feller, kept himself alive the whole winter. Don't know how he did it."

"How come you know him so well?"

"Oh, he comes around when I'm fishing, and I give him any too small for me to eat, or fish heads. He'll take fish heads. Take anything that smells like food. He's not fussy."

"So you're sort of like the summer people— feeding him."

The old man was silent, tensing up on his rod, reeling in a few inches, then letting it out again. Chad wished he had not let his tongue get away from him again. He had probably made the old guy mad. But before long the old man said, "Thing is, I'm here all year round. So he can depend on me giving him a handout pretty regular. Now the summer folks, they get him used to depending on them and then they up and leave him. There's the difference. See?"

"Yeah, I didn't think of it that way," Chad said.

The cat licked its paws delicately, first the topside of one, then turning it over, it licked the bottom.

"He's a proud little feller," the old man said. "Don't neglect his looks. Don't let himself get run down despite he lives alone—not like me. Of course, he's young yet."

"You live alone?"

"That's right. Got myself a box of a house just big enough to fit me and a bed. Used to be a shed, but I made it cozy with a good little stove. Nothing like a good, old-fashioned, wood-burning stove to keep you company cold winter nights. Hear the wind howling outside and them waves crashing against the cliffs so hard you think they're going to climb right over on top of you. But the stove—it'll crackle on just like a friend."

"Don't you have any family?"

"Got a daughter. She lives in California. Pretty girl—last I saw her. Of course, that was eight years ago now, and she's had three kids since. Last picture she sent me, I hardly recognized her. I suppose she'd say the same could she see me."

"Can't you go visit her?" Chad asked, but the old man got a bite just then.

"Feels like a big one," he said, twitching the rod up. He reeled in, then let the fish play the line out, reeled in again, concentrating as if bringing in the fish were serious business. The cat watched, as intent as the old man on what was happening. He doesn't have any money to visit her, Chad thought, answering his own question. Just the way not having any money was keeping April Anne and himself apart.

When the flat gray fish flipped out of the water onto the dock, the old man smacked it over the head with a heavy knife handle. Then he removed the baited hook from its gaping jaw.

"Good size for a flounder," he said. "Now I got me a start towards my dinner."

The two little kids with their father trailing behind them came over to see what had been caught. "Do you fish here often?" the father asked.

"Now and then," the old man said.

"Plenty of fish down there then?" the man asked.

"Maybe one or two is usually around."

"I don't know. This is the second day I've tried, and I haven't caught a thing. Maybe I'm using the wrong bait?"

"Maybe," the old man said.

"What do you use?"

"Whatever I got."

"Oh," the man said. "Well, thanks anyway."

"You're welcome," the old man said and turned his back toward the man and his children.

When they drifted off, Chad asked, "How come you didn't like him?"

The old man grinned. "How could you tell?"

"I could tell."

"He's a summer feller. Here today and gone to-morrow, takes what he can get and don't give nothing back. No sense wasting your breath on them."

"I'm only here for the summer," Chad said, testing.

"It's the type, not the length of stay," the old man said. He flipped another fish onto the splintery wood of the pier so fast Chad hadn't even known it was on the line. "Now this one here's the cat's dinner."

It was a small fish. The old man whacked it against the pier to kill it, then cut off its head and tossed the four-inch body and tail toward the cat. The cat jumped up to catch it before it flew back into the water. Holding the fish with one paw, the cat tore at the meat with the sharp, tusklike teeth on either side of its jaw. It fed in slow dignity, all the time watching the man and the boy, and licked its face with its furled flag of a red tongue.

"I wonder how he got food in the winter," Chad said.

"Garbage from the dump probably. Catch some field mice maybe—voles, moles, chipmunks, birds even. Maybe he's got another friend somewheres who feeds him. Only time I saw he got in trouble was when he tried to steal a sea gull's meal. That gull got so mad it chased the kitten clear down to the end of the dock pecking at him all the way. Would have killed him too if the cat hadn't been so smart."

"What'd he do?"

"Jumped overboard. Jumped right into the water and swam under the pier."

"I didn't know cats could swim."

"Usually they don't like to. Anyways, this cat swims when he has to."

"Did he get out by himself?"

"Well, I helped him some."

"Do you think he'll ever let me get close enough to pet him?"

"Doubt it. Don't know if anybody's ever touched that cat 'cepting when I helped him outta the water."

Chad moved closer to the cat and squatted. "Here kitty, here kitty, kitty . . ." He stretched out his hand slowly, palm up. The cat drew back against the piling; still holding the partially eaten fish with its paw, it arched its back and hissed.

Chad withdrew his hand. He would have to be patient, very patient, to win the cat's trust.

Toward noon, the old man began to pile his gear into a pickup truck as aged and disreputable-looking as himself.

"I'll come back tomorrow to see you if you're here," Chad said and waved good-bye. The old man waved in return. The cat had left as soon as it had eaten its fill of the fish.

Chad found the station wagon parked in front of the cottage and the family all in the living room.

"Where were you?" Roger demanded.

"Down by the pier in the marina."

"We were about to set out to look for you," Roger said.

"I saved you a sandwich from lunch," Pam said. "Tuna fish."

"I just took a walk," Chad said to Roger.

"You said you were going to stay around the cottage. When you make a commitment like that, I expect you to keep it."

"I'm sorry. I really didn't know it was so late. I only went for a walk."

"We've been home over an hour, Chad," Pam said. "Did you find anything interesting on your walk?"

"I met a fisherman. I was talking to him . . ."

"He doesn't have a watch," Polly said, joining her mother in Chad's defense.

"You'd better eat your sandwich," Pam said. "You must be hungry."

"Can we finally go hit some balls now, Dad?" Bob asked.

Roger hesitated. Then he shrugged, deciding not to make a big thing of it after all. He even said, "Want to come with us, Chad?"

Chad shook his head, wishing he could say Yes instead of No, but trying to play tennis was further than he wanted to go to appease Roger. "No, thanks," Chad said. "I really don't much like ball games."

"Well, suit yourself." Roger left, with Bob close on his heels.

"I'm going out do do my food shopping this afternoon," Pam said. "Anyone want to come along and help me?"

"I'll come, Mother," Polly said

"Can I come too?" Chad asked.

"Welcome!" Pam said with a smile.

Chapter 4

Chad was dreaming about money. He found a cache of coins in a hollow tree, but when he reached in to pick them up, they melted in his hands. The disappointment cut so deep he cried out and woke himself up. Still tangled in the dream, he wondered how would he ever get money to send his mother so she would believe he could take care of her.

The cracked plaster ceiling above him was unfamiliar, but then he never knew where he was when he woke up. It always took him a few minutes to figure it out. This time Bob's tennis racquet, propped against the wall in the corner of their bedroom, clued him in. The Sorenics. Cape Cod. Oh yeah! Chad swung his legs over the edge of the top bunk and dropped down to the painted wood floor. Gray sky showed in the top half of the bedroom window. Chad heard Polly and her mother talking in the kitchen and the sound of a screen door slamming. So he was the last one to get up this morning. He had overlsept.

"Hi," he said as he entered the kitchen after using the bathroom, remembering to wipe out the sink after brushing his teeth. Pam had explained they all did that, "as a courtesy to each other."

"Sleep well, Chad?" Pam asked with a smile for him.

"Fine." Chad had the feeling Pam would be glad to have him sit down and have a heart-to-heart talk with her, but he was not about to do it. He had never gotten anything from leaning on the sympathy of nice ladies like her except the jolt of having the supports pulled out from under him when they moved on, or when he did.

A creaking noise from overhead and a muffled curse made Chad glance up.

"Dad's fixing the roof. It leaks when it rains," Polly said.

Chad nodded. "He sure spends a lot of time fixing things." He poured himself a glass of juice and reached for the cereal box on a shelf.

"That's the price of our getting the cottage for the whole summer," Pam said. "My folks usually rent it out, and we only get it for a week before school starts, but this year the place needed so many repairs they offered it to us in exchange for Roger's labor.

Polly and I are going to paint the bedrooms and recover the couch and chair cushions. I may even make new curtains for the living room. What do you think, Polly?"

"See how it goes, Mom. Remember Grandma said the main thing she wanted you to do was get a good rest and put on some weight."

"Oh, Grandma always has worried about my weight. I'm in fine condition."

"You were sick all last winter."

"But I'm fine now."

"I'd like to help some," Chad heard himself offering.

"Why not?" Pam said. "You get involved wherever you feel comfortable, Chad. For a start, would you like to make the trip to the dump with Polly and me this morning?"

"Sure."

"We could use some muscle power on those boxes of rotten wood we have to load in the car."

To get to the dump they had to drive out to the main highway, follow it toward Provincetown for a way, turn left along a side road and then left again on another. "How far is this place?" Chad asked, surprised at the distance they had come.

"Not far as the crow flies, but a few miles if you have to stick to roads. Your cat probably does it in less than an hour."

"My cat?"

"The black-and-white cat you feed in the backyard every morning. Has he let you touch him yet?" Polly asked.

Caught in the act, Chad played it cool. "Not yet," he said. "Have you seen him at the dump?"

"I saw him there when I went with Dad the other morning. What do you call him?"

"Cat."

"You talk to him a lot," Pam said. "You must really love animals."

"Animals are okay—some of them. The people I lived with last summer had a dog used to sleep on the foot of my bed. I mean, he could've slept anywhere in the house, but he picked my bed."

"We might get a dog again. Couldn't we, Mom?"

"Nobody ever wanted to walk Boo," Pam said. "It's a problem with the leash law now."

"Boo was an airedale," Polly said. "He got killed when a car hit him in front of our house last year."

"That's pretty bad. You must have felt rotten," Chad said.

"Yes. We all cried, even Dad."

"Your father cried?"

Pam laughed. "He may sound like a gruff old top sergeant, but he's really softhearted, Chad."

"A poo bear," Polly said, grinning at some private family joke.

The dump looked like a moon landscape, except that the series of bare mounds occasionally erupted

41

in rashes of garbage. Where the biodegradable paper bags of scraps, melon rinds, and coffee grounds were exposed, gulls by the hundreds cruised overhead, frequently landing to pick something out. One area was set aside for metal and glass objects, old rusted cars, and bedsprings all heaped together.

"That's where I saw your cat." Polly said, pointing toward a pile of car bodies.

Chad reached to haul out the boxes of wood by himself when Pam opened the back of the wagon. "Hey, that's not a one-man operation!" she said.

"I'm stronger than I look." Chad was proud to be able to handle the boxes alone. He noticed a man shoving garbage into a hole with the big blade of a bulldozer. The man leaned out the window of the cab holding what looked like a stick until he lifted the thing to his shoulder and aimed. Then Chad saw it was a gun. The sound of the shot was muffled by the dozer's engine.

"What's that man shooting at?" Chad asked.

"I don't know," Polly replied. "That's weird."

"Let's get out of here before he points that thing at us," Pam said. "I don't like guns."

"Me either," Polly agreed. They both helped Chad with the rest of the load, hurrying to get away. When the next shot came, Pam was behind the wheel in the driver's seat and Polly was sliding in next to her. The bullet went right past their windshield.

"Chad, get in. He's a maniac!" Pam screeched.

But Chad had seen what the man was shooting at. The cat, *his* cat, had streaked past the car and dived into the warren of junked cars.

"He's trying to kill my cat! Hey you, hey you on the dozer!" Chad was shouting as he ran up the dirt hill nearest the car and stood on the top so that the man, who was in the next flat area over, would notice him.

"Chad, come back here!" Pam was crying. Chad could just barely hear her over the noise of her racing car engine and the rumble of the bulldozer. Pam cut the engine back to idle but didn't back the car out. Chad raced down the other side of the hill and charged over to the bulldozer. "Hey you!" he yelled up at the man in it, a big, square-jawed guy with black hair hanging in his eyes. "Hey you, why're you shooting at that cat?"

The man stared down at Chad vacantly. His mouth hung open. He looked freaky, freaky but dangerous with the gun still in his hands. For a minute the man stared down at him without answering, then he lowered the gun down inside the cab somewhere and put the dozer in motion. He looked back over his shoulder once at Chad as he went back to moving the mounds of garbage around. Chad caught his breath; he had been breathing hard. He ran over the hill to the car.

"Wow, are you brave!" Polly said.

"Foolhardy is the word for it," Pam said, sounding upset. "You could have been killed."

"You waited for me," Chad observed.

"Well, I certainly wasn't going to go off and leave you there alone with that crazy man."

"Your mother's the brave one," Chad said to Polly.

"Oh, I know she is," Polly said. "She's an all-round terrific lady."

"What a way to earn a compliment," Pam said. "I'm still shaking." She drove them home very slowly. "I'm going to ask Roger to find out what can be done about that man. He shouldn't be allowed to carry a gun like that."

"Yeah," Chad agreed. The odds on his cat continuing to escape a man with a gun did not seem too high. Sooner or later the man wasn't going to miss.

Chapter 5

Later on that morning Chad offered the cat the piece of hamburger he had saved from last night's dinner. He offered it from his fingers, not from a bowl. The cat came close enough to take it, then withdrew and ate it from the ground, eyeing Chad between bites and swallows. Chad remained crouched in the same position with his fingers extended. When it finished the meat, the cat crept back warily and sniffed Chad's fingers. Then Chad crooked one finger out and stroked the cat's throat. As if it had always been petted, the cat tilted its head back and leaned into Chad's fingers. Chad smiled with pleasure.

When the cat ran off down the backside of the hill finally, Chad followed after it as well as he could through the low-growing, twisty scrub oak and pine and berry bushes. Every place open to the sun was filled with small-leaved bearberry and bayberry bushes. Poison ivy blended in so well with the other ground covers that Chad was in the middle of a patch of it before he realized it.

Picking his way out of the poison ivy, Chad didn't see the house until he was right on the edge of the lawn. It was a real house, not weathered gray like the Sorenics' cottage, but painted white with blue shutters, surrounded by a flower garden and fancied up with long-legged pink ceramic birds. An old lady straightened up from her bent-over position in the garden bed where she had been weeding.

"What do you want, boy?" She wore a sun hat tied under her chin and glasses that magnified her eyes enormously. Her mouth was only a slit sunk in her wrinkles.

"Nothing," Chad said.

"Where do you come from?" She held a three-pronged weeding tool in her hand like a spear.

"The other side of the hill." He pointed. "Sorenics' cottage."

"Sorenics? You mean the Richards."

"I don't know. The Sorenics have it for the summer."

"Must be his name. Her parents are the Richards. She was a Richard before she got married. Did you say the whole summer?"

Chad nodded. She was a nosey old lady.

"Well, that's news. And what are you planning to

do with yourself for the whole summer, young man?"

"Me?"

"Are you going to spend all your time playing, or would you like some work to do?"

"I'd like some work if I was getting paid for it," Chad answered. Even if he didn't like her, he would work for her if she paid him.

"Well, if you're any kind of worker, I can use you. Pay you a dollar an hour for helping me in the garden."

A dollar an hour. That wasn't much, but it was sure better than nothing. "What do you want me to do?"

"Just now the weeds are getting ahead of me. Can you tell a weed from a flower?"

"Not too good," Chad admitted.

"Well, I'll show you." She directed him to the bushel basket she was filling. "Anything that looks like this or this or this, you pull out." She showed him three samples of weeds. "Start at that corner of the house and work toward me. I'll get you a basket."

A cat startled him when it brushed against his knees while he was concentrating on yanking up weeds with roots attached. This cat was a huge fluffy gray monster with a head twice the size of *his* cat's head.

"That's Lord Elgin," the lady said proudly. "He's my companion."

"He's big."

"Gentle as a kitten though."

Lord Elgin left to stalk a bird. Chad had just finished filling his first basket, working as fast as he could go to prove to the lady what a hard worker he was, when he heard the yowling. It was an eerie, heart-stopping sound.

"At it again, are you?" the old woman screeched. "I'll teach you to come sneaking around here you . . ." She picked up a fist-sized rock and waddled rapidly over to where Lord Elgin and the black-and-white cat were hissing at each other with arched backs. At a distance of two feet from the cats, she threw the rock at the black-and-white cat. It dodged agilely and ran up a tree. Safe in the tree, the cat stretched out on a lower limb and looked down at them.

"Here, boy," the old woman said. "Maybe your aim is better. See if you can hit that black cat for me."

"I will not," Chad said indignantly.

"Why not?"

"He's not doing anything to you. He's . . ."

"He's nothing but an alley cat, probably full of vermin and disease. If Lord Elgin ever gets bitten by him, I'll have to take him to the vet for all kinds of shots."

"Lord Elgin is twice as big as him."

"Lord Elgin happens to be a valuable cat. He's Persian, and besides, he's fourteen years old. That's getting on for a cat."

"I think I better stop working for you now," Chad said. "The Sorenics get mad when they don't know where I am."

"How long have you been working?" the old lady asked. "Half an hour?"

Chad looked at the sun and down at the basket he had filled. "At least an hour," he said.

"Well," the old lady grumbled. "That's stretching it a bit. But all right. You come back to do some more weeding tomorrow then, and I'll pay you."

She was a sharp dealer, Chad thought, not surprised because she looked mean to him. He had been gypped by people like her before. Let them run up a bill, and then it was his word against theirs about how much they owed him. "I'd like to have my dollar now," Chad said. "I'll come back tomorrow anyway. I promise."

The old woman looked at him hard and sniffed. "My name is Mrs. Saugerty, and I'm in the phone book. You can trust me, boy."

"My name is Chad Lester, and I live down in the Sorenics' cottage. You can trust me too."

"Well, I don't happen to have a dollar on me now."

Chad looked at her without saying anything. He

didn't believe her for a minute. If she didn't pay him, he would just not come back tomorrow no matter how much he needed the money. The last time he had been cheated, it had put him in such a tearing rage that he had broken a chair in the Children's Shelter and had to do latrine duty forever to pay for it. He was not going to get himself into a fix like that again if he could help it.

"All right," the old woman said grudgingly. "I'll go see if I have some change somewhere in the house. Could be I do." She went inside, closing the door behind her.

Probably she's afraid I'll steal her money if I knew she has any, he thought—an old lady alone in the woods. But she was so mean about the cat. She didn't deserve sympathy. Nevertheless, if she paid him, he would come back to work for her. He wondered why the cat came by here if it knew it was going to get rocks thrown at it. Shot at and almost hit with a rock all in one day! It was amazing that the cat had survived a whole year.

Mrs. Saugerty came waddling out of the house finally with a handful of change, favoring one leg as she came down the steps.

"Thank you," he said when she dumped the change into his hand. Just the same he counted it before putting it in his pocket. It *was* a dollar.

"You are *not* a nice boy," she said with a prim mouth.

"Do you want me to come back tomorrow anyway?"

Mrs. Saugerty glanced toward the bushel basket full of weeds he had pulled and said, "Might as well."

Chad ran top speed through the underbrush and got back just as the Sorenics were sitting down to lunch. He had been pulling weeds for way over an hour, but at least nobody gave him a hard time about where he had been all morning.

"It should be beautiful over at the ocean side this afternoon," Pam said to Roger.

"Get in enough practice to suit you this morning, Bob?" Roger asked his son.

"I hit that ball three hundred and ten times in a row against the backboard before I missed." Bob was piling up cheese and meat and mayonnaise and lettuce to make a sandwich.

"Not bad. If you can hit a thousand by the end of the summer, you'll be getting there. Okay, what say we all go to the ocean till late this afternoon, and then Bob and I will play a little tennis before dinner?"

"Sounds good to me," Polly said.

"I'd like to go with you, if that's okay," Chad said.

"Sure," Roger replied, sounding pleased. "Glad to have you."

Chad was surprised that the man should be pleased so easily. Maybe Pam was right. Maybe he was softer than he sounded.

In the car Pam reminded her husband, "Don't forget you were going to stop at town hall and talk to them about that man at the dump."

"Oh, right. I'll swing through town, and we can stop right now."

The town was nothing much, a narrow main street jammed with tourists and banks and little shops. The town hall, a white clapboard building larger than the rest, sat in front of a couple of acres of black asphalt parking lot with a fish market tucked in one back corner of it. Roger parked between one car with a surfboard upside down on top and another car with a surfboard sticking out its rear door. "Be right back," he said.

"Don't you want me to go with you?" Pam asked.

"Not necessary. This will only take a minute."

Half an hour later, when they were all miserable from the heat inside the car, Roger returned. He slammed the door as he got in and didn't look at Pam as he said, "Well, I filed a complaint. They told me there'd been a lot of complaints. Seems the fellow uses the rifle to shoot rats—also anything else that moves that he feels like blasting away at."

"And?" Pam asked. "Are they going to make him stop?"

"Seems they can't. I can bring the matter up before the town board if I want. The only hitch is they don't meet again until September."

"Oh," Pam said. "They gave you the old run around, huh? Well, at least you tried, Roger."

"The only thing I can see to do is I'll take the stuff to the dump myself from now on."

Nobody said anything about his cat. Chad seethed. So Roger was not the big-shot fixer he acted like! It figured. People talked about fixing rotten things but they never *did* anything about them, nothing that changed anything. The cat would have to be lucky, that was all. He stared out the window and anger gnawed at his belly as the bushy pines whisked monotonously by.

In the beach parking lot the sun glittered off the roof of every car. The sky overhead was a solid block of robin's-egg-blue and, below the dunes, the gleaming, pale green water broke in gentle curls of foam against the beach.

"Last one in is a rotten egg," Bob yelled as he dumped his share of the family's equipment and dashed into the water, diving through the first wave. Roger looked at Chad inquiringly.

"Coming in, Chad?"

"In a while maybe." He figured he would try it today. It was hard even to remember what had scared him about the ocean that first time he saw it. Had it really growled in all dark green and ragged-looking? Had it looked so mean or had he imagined it?

Chad lay on his stomach, letting the hot sun massage his back and feeling his mood change for the better. When Polly said, "I think I'll go in for a dip, Mom," he sat up.

"I'm coming with you, Polly."

They passed Roger and Bob, running up the slope dripping water and looking well chilled. "How come you don't go in with your father and brother?" Chad asked Polly.

"Oh, them! All they do is zoom around the water like speedboats. I like to just stand around and jump waves. Just lazy, I guess."

"Me too," Chad said. Despite his determination not to get attached to any of them, he couldn't help liking Polly. She was such a neat kid. He stayed beside her patiently as she inched herself into the frigid water.

The waves were just high enough to lift them up gently and set them back with their feet on the bottom. They jumped waves and swam a few strokes. Polly admired Chad's suntan and bemoaned her own red, peeling nose. A kid on a surf raft lost his ball and Chad swam after it for him. "You're a good swimmer," Polly said.

"Oh, I'm not much. Just used to pools mostly."

He and Polly had just come out of the water when Roger said, "Time for some jogging, Bob. Up and at 'em."

"Ah, Dad, let me be. I'm sleeping," Bob mumbled, lying on his stomach with his head under his arm.

"How are you going to be a tennis pro if you lie around all summer getting fat? Come on!"

"Ask Chad. He can run with you. Unless he hates that too."

"I'll run with you," Chad said to Roger.

Roger flipped his son over and kicked sand at him. "Come on then, Chad," he said, taking off fast to escape Bob's fury. Chad followed on Roger's heels. Bob, howling with rage, was soon up and after them. Roger could really run, Chad thought. He found the sand hard going and allowed the man's muscular form to get farther and farther ahead of him. After all, he's a gym teacher so he should be in good shape, Chad comforted himself. Bob caught up with Chad and ran beside him for a while, puffing a little to Chad's surprise.

"How come . . ." Bob panted, "you're running with us . . . instead of hanging around . . . with your girl friend?"

"What girl friend?" Chad asked.

"My sister, Polly . . . either you got a crush . . . on her . . . or," he puffed, "you're a fag."

"I don't have a crush on anybody," Chad said. "And I'm no fag either."

"Then how come . . . you're always hanging around . . . with Mom and Polly and . . . your kitty?"

"Maybe they're the only ones round here worth my time," Chad snapped. "What's so tough about you anyway? Hitting a tennis ball all day doesn't make you tough."

"I'm going out for football too . . . this fall."

"Oh, big man! You really think you're a hotshot, don't you? Just like your father!"

Bob stopped running and grabbed Chad's arm, pulling him up short.

"Let go!" Chad said.

"What'd you say about my dad?"

"Nothing. Except you and him are not the hotshots you think you are, that's all."

Bob shoved him so hard that Chad fell back, landing on his elbows in the sand. He was up in an instant. He rammed his head into Bob's gut. Street fighting was something he knew more about than tennis. Even though Bob outweighed him by thirty pounds and was a head taller, Chad was not afraid of him. He had Bob down in the sand and was bending his fingers back when Roger turned back and saw the fight.

"Hey, you guys!" Roger shouted from twenty yards down the beach. "What do you think you're doing?"

Chad let Bob go and sprang back. Now he was in for it! Roger would cream him for beating up his kid. Chad looked around anxiously. No place to escape. He knew the smart thing to do would be to lie low until Roger had a chance to cool down, but where could he go? The water was out—they could swim faster and longer than he could. The dunes here were high and steep as office buildings. He could make it back to Pam and Polly, but he wasn't about to ask for protection from women. No way out. He straightened up, preparing to take whatever punishment Roger dished out.

"What were you two beating on each other about?" Roger asked, not even winded as he drew up alongside them.

"Nothing," Bob mumbled.

"What do you mean, nothing? I asked a question. Answer it." Roger's voice was hard.

"I said something he didn't like so he said something back," Bob said.

"And?"

"And I started it."

"I see. And got the worst of it, huh?"

"Yeah."

"Well, are you going to apologize to Chad before or after I make you?"

"I'm sorry, Chad," Bob said.

"That's okay," Chad said, barely able to believe his ears. The guy had been fair! Roger hadn't assumed that Bob was right and that Chad was a trouble maker. And Bob hadn't lied and stuck it all on Chad. He had to admit it; they were both pretty decent. Chad looked at Roger with respect for the first time.

Chapter 6

All that week the sun polished their days to a glossy brilliance and everybody seemed cheerful. Chad rose early to run with Bob and Roger down along the harbor beach past the marina and back—two miles—before breakfast. His appetite improved so much that he put on a few pounds. Pam told him he was looking terrific. He felt good. He worked a couple of mornings for the old lady, Mrs. Saugerty, and was just biding his time until he could write to his mother and send her his earnings.

Mrs. Saugerty had turned out to be a very chatty lady. All the while he worked, she puttered around talking at him. Mostly she talked about her children, who were middle-aged people in their forties. One set of children was coming for a visit soon, bringing their children who were all of college age. Mrs. Saugerty did not sound as if she approved of her grandchildren very much. She criticized her own children too; how her daughter-in-law had gotten too fat and her son didn't save his money—things like that. Chad wished he could turn her off, but knew better than to tell her to shut up.

The cat was beginning to act as if he enjoyed being petted. He sometimes came up and thrust his head out to be scratched. No purr yet, but he would hang around Chad for ten or fifteen minutes after his morning breakfast, just playing around. He'd roll onto his side and wait until Chad was within inches of touching him, then streak off into the underbrush. In a couple of minutes he'd prance back, right up to Chad's feet, bouncing sideways on all four legs with his back arched. Sometimes he would bat at Chad's fingers with his claws properly retracted as if he understood that Chad's skin was fragile stuff. Chad tried not to think about the guy with the gun in the dump. Most of the time he succeeded.

Chester, the old man on the pier, was feeling good too. The minute Chad arrived Thursday morning, the old man told him proudly, "My daughter wrote me. Says she's saving up to come for a visit. Going to take some special fare deal and fly here by plane end of August if it all works out."

"With her kids?"

"No. No, she can't afford to bring the kids this time. Her husband is just a sailor. She's got a friend who's going to keep the kids for her. Then likely she'll do the same for the friend come her turn for vacation. How about that, Chad? Here's she's been saving her pennies all this time to come see her old father, and she never even told me."

"Maybe she was worried she wouldn't be able to save enough."

"Right, right. You're a smart kid. She's been cleaning some lady's house for her to pick up the extra. Isn't that something? I didn't think I'd get to see her again. Used to get me down thinking about how I might pass on without seeing her again, you know?"

"Yeah," Chad said. "I can believe it."

"Well, how's your cat doing?"

"Good. Nobody's shot at him or hit him in the head with a rock for a few days. Say, Chester, do you know the guy in the dump that shoots at everything with his rifle?"

"You mean the crazy? Got a big jaw, never talks?"

"That's him."

"Yeah, I know him as much as I have to. Best keep a distance from that fellow. He kills things for kicks."

"He'd like to kill my cat. I think my cat lives in the dump."

"Probably. Probably found himself a cozy berth out of the elements in there. Well, best you can do is hope the cat is smarter than Jackson."

"Jackson's the guy's name?"

———

"That's right. His father's a big man in this town. That's why they let Jackson run the bulldozer at the dump. Keeps him out of mischief, well, most of the time, anyhow."

It was hopeless, Chad thought. All he could do was keep his fingers crossed for the cat.

"How would it be," Chester said, "if I bring some extra fishing gear along and let you try your luck?"

"That'd be neat." Chad was pleased, because the old man really had to like him to make an offer like that.

Everything was going so well that Chad decided the moment had come to write his mother. That evening he borrowed a pencil and paper from Pam. "If I write a letter, will you mail it for me?"

"Sure, Chad."

"I mean, check the address and everything to make sure I do it right?"

"Who are you writing to?"

"My mother."

"Good idea."

Armed with a pencil with a good point and another with a good eraser, Chad sat down at the kitchen table face to face with a blank sheet of paper. As if in sympathy with the paper, his mind went blank too. He could whip off answers to questions in workbooks or the short-answer tests teachers were

61

always giving in school easily enough, but he was not used to dealing with so much unmapped space. He rolled the pencil around on his lip for a while, tried to balance it loose on his upper lip, dropped it, and had to crawl around under the table after it.

"Having trouble getting started, Chad?" Pam asked sympathetically.

"Yeah."

"Why don't you say how you like it here, and then start telling her the kinds of things you do during the days."

"Like what?"

"Like swimming and running. Oh, and you could tell her about how you're taming the cat."

"Yeah, thanks," Chad said. If he started like that though, he would never get to the point of the letter. The happy memory came to him, the early one when he'd lived with his mother. They would sit on the stoop together watching the world go by—dogs lifting their legs at the fire hydrant, big kids on bicycles, ladies with shopping carts, garbage trucks. Sitting on the stoop was all he could remember of that time before he was five; that and his mother's arm soft around his shoulders and the tickle of her talking in his ear. He finally wrote:

Dear Mom,
I saved some money for you. I erned it doing yard work for an old lady over the other side of the hill

here. She's not the nicest old lady, but I don't let her cheat me much. I can ern more money doing odd jobs when you and me find a place where there's stores around and things. I'm old enough to work now. I can support you pretty good, and I don't mind working hard because you and me can be together then, so you don't have to marry that guy you wrote about. I'll even go to church with you on Sundays—once in a while anyway. That is if I don't have a job Sundays like cutting lawns or shuvling snow. I gained a few pounds and I look and feel strong as an ox. If you can't come here to get me, just let me know where to come, and I'll come to you. I miss you a whole lot.

Your loving son,
Chad

He read over what he had written, asked Pam how to spell "shoveling" and "earned," crossed the misspelled words out and respelled them correctly. The letter sounded all right, but suppose—suppose his mama had acted fast this time instead of taking forever to do something as she usually did. Suppose she had already married the guy! Chad shook himself. No sense thinking that way. But it was good he had written the letter tonight. If it got in the mail tomorrow, he felt certain it would reach her in time. He took his money from the dirty sock hidden in his duffle bag, tucked it in between the folds of the letter, and sealed the envelope. Then he went to Pam for help in addressing it. While Pam was looking for a stamp, Polly said,

"I think I'm going for a walk, Mom."

"Where to?"

"Oh, just along the harbor."

Chad heard a sadness in Polly's voice. She had kept her distance from him lately, hadn't spent much time with him all week. Why? It could be Bob had been teasing her about being Chad's girl friend the way he teased Chad. That could be it. If so, it was stupid. Stupid to let people tease you out of anything you wanted. Chad had learned that when he was four years old, when he let them drown his teddy bear to show them he wasn't a baby. He could not remember the names of those kids now, but they had all been foster kids—all much older than he.

That was right after his mother got sick and couldn't take care of him anymore, and they had sent him off to his first foster home. He remembered the lady in that house, and her big booming laugh that scared him at first. But she used to hold him in her arms in her rocking chair at night when he cried for his mama. He had stayed there nearly a year. It would not have been too bad a place if the older kids had not picked on him so much. "Cry baby—little baby—mama's boy," they had singsonged at him. He cried all the time that year, so stupid he didn't know tears just invited their meanness.

"Hey," Chad said as Polly went out the door. "Mind if I go with you?"

"Why no." Polly looked surprised.

Chad followed her outside before anyone had time to comment. The sky was rouging up for evening, all blotched with pink above the trees. They crossed the road and passed between two cottages to get to the harbor beach. The pink sky had a pale green border spotted with irregular puffs of lavendar clouds. The water was streaked with color as if the dyes from the sunset had run onto its silvery surface. An extra stillness surrounded them, and they spoke in undertones to match the evening.

"This is my favorite time of day," Polly said. "It's so fantastically beautiful."

"Yeah," Chad said. "It's nice. Hey, Polly? Are you mad at me about something?"

"Why should I be mad at you?"

"I don't know. I haven't seen you much."

"You're the one who's been busy all week."

Chad considered. What with working for Mrs. Saugerty and spending time with the cat and with Chester and with Bob and Roger, he had been busy.

"Well," he said. "What've *you* been doing?"

"What else? Helping mother, reading, wishing I were somebody else."

"What do you mean? Why would you want to be anybody else?" He was shocked. He often wished he could be better or stronger or smarter, but never did he want to be anybody but Chad Lester.

Polly was embarrassed. "Oh, you know. I imagine how it would be if I were some person in a book instead of me."

"What's wrong with being you?"

"Well, except that I'm too big and fat and ugly, and it makes me sick to my stomach when I have to go into a new place or meet people, and I never can think of anything to say to anyone outside the family—nothing's wrong with me." She sighed. "There, that's what you get for asking dumb questions—dumb answers. Right?" Polly was trying to be flippant about it but Chad was not fooled. She had meant every word.

"Polly," he said. "I bet you nobody's like the people in books, and even if they are, there aren't many people nicer than you."

"How do you know?" she challenged him. "You don't know me very well."

"Yes, I do," he said. "I know a lot about people. That's one thing I know—people. I've met all kinds."

"I guess."

"So you better believe me. You're okay, except maybe you're a little shy."

She smiled and her freckled face became warm as a toasted bun. "If you say so," she said.

He grinned back. "Now, tell me what you've been reading."

"One book was about this orphan boy and his dog who run away together. He reminded me of you a little . . ."

"I'm no orphan."

"No. But you have the cat though, and I heard Mom talking to Dad about something the caseworker said—that was before I met you—I mean, you know about it, don't you?"

"About what?"

"About your mother saying you could be adopted now?"

"My mother never said that!"

Polly was clearly embarrassed. "I'm sorry. I mean, I just thought I heard Mom say that your caseworker said your mother signed some papers and sent you a letter. I guess I misunderstood."

"It's not true. My mother would never give me up for adoption!"

"She wouldn't?"

"Of course not. See, Mom says a lot of things, but it's all talk. She doesn't really mean them except just while she's saying them. Then she forgets or she changes her mind right away. See?"

"No." Polly looked at him, puzzled.

"Like she'll promise to come see me, and she wants to, but then she can't get away or something. But she means well. She wouldn't give me up for adoption. One time she did say maybe I'd be better off if she could make herself give me up to some nice couple who'd bring me up right and send me off to college and all, but she said she never could give me up. See, I'm all she has."

"How old were you then, when she said that?" Polly asked.

"I was . . . I don't know. We were in a playground. She bought me a sand pail and shovel, and I was— oh, a little kid, I guess." It upset him to realize how long ago that had been. Then there was the letter this summer, the one he had read so many times and hadn't understood. But she didn't mean it. Even if she said it, she didn't mean it. They walked without talking until Polly pointed at the water and said, "Look!"

Out in the water fish were jumping, making flashing arcs of light. "There's another," Chad said. They watched, but the brief spectacle was over. When they started walking again, Polly asked, "What's your mother like?"

"She's just—you know. She's soft and pretty. She's got this delicate skin that gets all red in the sunlight like yours . . . she's—it's hard to describe your own mother."

"Does she have a job?"

"Yeah, she works. Sometimes. She had a job in a supermarket as a checkout girl last year. That was when she told me she was going to take me to live with her now that I was old enough to take care of myself when she went out."

"Then what happened?"

"I don't know. She said the manager didn't like her, or she gave the wrong change or something. Anyway, she lost that job."

"You must have been awfully disappointed."

"Not me. See, she's always promising me things, and I know not to count on it too much. Like she says she will and she *wants* to, but then things happen and she can't. She always feels as bad as me about it. That's why I'm not worrying about her letting me go for adoption now."

"But if she never can take care of you, wouldn't you be better off getting a permanent family instead of moving around so much?" Polly frowned. "I'd hate having to get used to a new family all the time like you do. I couldn't stand it."

"Nobody wants to adopt a kid my age anyway. I mean, even if I wanted to be adopted—which I don't."

"It's so hard," Polly said.

"Anyway, now I can take care of her," Chad said. "I'm old enough. That's what I wrote to tell her— that she won't have to marry that man now."

"You're a strong person, Chad. I really admire you. I'm glad the agency sent us you instead of the girl my mother asked for."

"Your mother wanted a girl?" Chad stopped short in dismay, ignoring the complimentary part of what Polly had said. "Why'd she want a girl?"

Polly was embarrassed. She watched the toe of her sneaker dig a hole in the hard wet sand before she answered. "She thought I should have a girl to spend time with me. Dad thinks I read too much."

"Your dad does?"

"He says kids are supposed to socialize with each other. According to him, I'm the only girl my age who doesn't have a telephone growing out of her ear."

"That's dumb. It's good you're not just like every other girl. You don't go around giggling about people or acting stuck-up. Girls are mostly boring."

"Well, I'm boring. I even bore myself sometimes."

Chad didn't know what to say to that. He himself did not get bored.

"And," Polly continued, "Dad says I have to overcome my shyness. He says that's my worst problem."

"What's your father, some kind of expert on how kids are supposed to be?"

"Well, he and Mom read all these psychology books. Being shy is supposed to be bad for you, like having a disease."

"I don't think you're too shy."

"I am with most people—not with you though."

"How come?" The incoming dark was sealing them off from the rest of the world. Chad was no longer hurt at not being first choice with the Sorenics. He was too full of warmth for this sweet, solid girl who liked him, even said she admired *him*—Chad Thomas Lester.

"I don't know," Polly was saying. "I guess it's because you don't make fun of me. You don't tease me the way Bob does, either."

"Bob's just a kid. He'll grow out of it."

Far out where the purple edge of the water met the somber blue of the darkening sky, the triangle of a ship sat outlined with pinpricks of light. It was strange, Chad thought, how beautiful the world looked when he was with Polly.

They walked side by side toward the neon signs of the restaurants and shops of the marina. "I brought money for ice cream," Polly said.

"I don't have any money," Chad said.

"That's okay. I'll treat."

"No thanks." He had sent all his money to his mother. He couldn't return her treat.

Polly bought two ice creams at the day-bright window of the soft-ice cream stand, one chocolate, one vanilla. She held them out toward Chad. "Pick which one you want."

"I don't want any."

"I'll have to throw one away then."

"Boy, are you stubborn!" he said.

"Same as you."

They grinned at each other. He took the chocolate. "Thanks." Polly was his friend. He hadn't had a friend in a long time, not a real one, one who didn't need him for protection or something. He'd like to buy her a gift, maybe that key chain with the whistle on it that he'd seen at the tackle shop. It only cost a dollar fifty. Tomorrow he'd go see if Mrs. Saugerty had any more work for him to do.

"You two look happy," Pam said when they walked into the cottage.

"We had a nice walk," Chad said. Polly was smiling. To his surprise, he was too.

Chapter 7

Last minute preparations for the arrival of her children had Mrs. Saugerty excited She hobbled around breathlessly giving Chad orders. "Now, don't forget I want all those lawn chairs brought out after you finish scrubbing the birdbath, and don't dump that soapy water near my dahlias. It won't do them any good. I wish I could send you to the store for me. I forgot the dill."

"The what?"

"Dill. It's good in salad. Didn't you ever have any?"

"No."

"Well, that's right. You're a deprived child; so it's no wonder. I met your Mrs. Sorenic in the market yesterday. She told me about you being a foster child. *You* never told me that."

"You never asked."

"Don't be fresh . . . I want everything looking just so when John comes. His wife notices things. She comes from a prominent Philadelphia family. They—"

"Where do you want the water dumped?" Chad asked, having scrubbed the shallow stone birdbath clean.

"In the woods, of course."

Chad struggled with the heavy stone bowl, slopping half the water out before he got it to the edge of the lawn where the woods began. Mrs. Saugerty stood there with her hands on her hips clucking disapprovingly at him. He would get a lot more done, and so would she, he thought, if she went about her business instead of standing around bugging him all the time.

"That cat!" Mrs. Saugerty said. "Here he is again. Wicked beast! Scat!" She scuttled over to her garden hose, turned it on full blast, and aimed it at the cat which slipped back into the woods.

"He's not doing anything to you," Chad protested. "What are you always chasing him for?"

"I'm going to do worse than chase him if he doesn't stop coming around bothering Lord Elgin."

"He doesn't hurt Lord Elgin."

"He gets right up on the windowsill and peers in at him. Gets Lord Elgin so frantic he claws my curtains. I spent all yesterday afternoon repairing the tears he made."

"That's not the cat's fault."

74

"No? And I found a dead goldfinch with its parts eaten out, by the bird feeder yesterday afternoon too."

"Maybe Lord Elgin killed it."

"Lord Elgin gets chopped chicken livers for dinner or minced fish. He doesn't care to eat birds."

Chad stopped arguing. It was useless anyway. He went down into the basement which had lift-up wooden doors as an outside entryway. It was hard to drag the redwood-colored lawn chairs up the concrete steps and out onto the lawn alone, but he managed.

After he brought out the round table that stood between the chairs, Mrs. Saugerty said, "I told my son John to bring me some rat poison . . . Put that chair more toward the tree, Chad . . . I could fix that cat once and for all if I mixed the poison with some of Lord Elgin's chicken livers and left it at the edge of the woods."

"You couldn't be *that* mean!" Chad was too horrified to be discreet.

"Mean? You think I'm *mean*? What gives you the right to call me mean?" Mrs. Saugerty glared at him, and her face got so red that Chad was afraid she might have an attack of some kind. Not that he cared, but he didn't want to be blamed for it.

"It's mean to go around killing innocent cats that don't have anybody but themselves to take care of them. That cat's not doing you any harm. Why can't you just leave him alone?"

"And why can't *you* mind your own business, young man?"

"It *is* my business. That cat is mine." He bit his lip. There he went again, jumping into the fire instead of playing it cool.

"Yours? It's your cat? Since when?"

"He comes to me every morning. I feed him. I'm the only one can touch him."

"Feeding doesn't make him yours. Touching doesn't either."

"What does then?"

The question stopped her for a minute. Then the answer burst out of her in triumph. "Dependence! It's yours if it's dependent on you."

Chad slammed down the chair he was holding. "Is this where you want this?"

"I don't like your attitude today, young man. I don't like it at all. And it's none of your business what I do with that cat." Mrs. Saugerty looked at Chad, prim-mouthed. "I was going to give you a little extra today, but I don't know if I should now, considering your fresh mouth."

She paid him just what she owed him and he set back over the hill, fuming. She was the most purely hateful woman he had ever met. Now the cat was in danger not only from the man in the dump but from

Mrs. Saugerty. Chad churned over ideas for rescue. None of them seemed promising.

"What's the matter?" Polly asked, looking up from her book as he stalked into the kitchen.

"Nothing except now Mrs. Saugerty's going to kill my cat!"

Chapter 8

The cat gave a wide-mouthed, weak-voiced cry to announce its arrival at the pine tree, but Chad was too busy figuring out what to do about Mrs. Saugerty to pay attention. The cat butted its head under Chad's arm and pushed hard against his side. "We got problems, Cat," Chad told him. The trusting amber eyes remained calm. The cat meowed, kneading Chad's leg with claws extended. "Hey, watch it, you!" Chad complained.

He distracted the cat with a pinecone. Tail twitching, the cat lay back on Chad's leg and batted the pinecone with one front paw. When Chad tossed the cone, the cat leaped after it and rolled on its back, clutching the cone to its belly with all four paws. It looked up at Chad through half-crossed eyes, pink tongue tipped out. Chad laughed out loud.

"You sound happy," Polly said, joining Chad under the pine tree. She had a dish in her hand.

"I'm going to see if he'll let me touch him today."

"I'm not really happy," Chad said. "I came up here to think, and the cat started clowning around."

"He's an awfully cute cat."

"Going to be a dead one soon if I don't figure out a way to save him."

The bowl Polly held out to the cat was full of scraps from last night's dinner—rice and eggs and tomatoes and green peppers. The cat walked boldly up to the bowl and sat there looking at Polly. She picked out a chunk of omelet and offered it. The cat averted its head as if it were not interested. Polly let the tidbit drop back into the bowl. The cat licked its flank, washing the already glossy black hair with the rough sponge of its tongue. Seeing it occupied with its toilet, Polly sat back, crossing her legs comfortably under her and pulling the heavy locks of her long red hair over her shoulders. Immediately, the cat snaked its head at the bowl and began to gobble down the food as if someone might grab it away.

"Look at that!" Polly said. "What an actor! I really thought he didn't want it."

"Yeah," Chad said gloomily. "And that's how he'll get himself killed this weekend when Mrs. Saugerty sets out her poisoned bait. He'll gobble down anything without even sniffing it."

"No, he won't. Cats are too smart to eat poisoned food."

"Not him. He eats everything," Chad said, as the cat licked up the last of the rice and peppers.

"You could keep him inside the cottage over the weekend," Polly suggested.

"How would I make him stay? He's never been inside. Besides, she'll probably have enough poison to try more than just one weekend."

"Why don't you ask Mom and Dad? They'll come up with something."

Chad did not think much of that idea. Adults had never been any use in solving his problems; more often they caused them. But no better idea came to him, so he tried it.

Sure enough, the suggestion Pam came up with was no good. "Why don't I go have a talk with Mrs. Saugerty and tell her what the cat means to you. I'm sure she wouldn't deliberately hurt you, Chad."

"I already told her the cat is mine and that I feed him."

"I bet you didn't explain so that she understands how you feel. I can't believe she'd deliberately harm someone else's pet—a stray maybe, but a pet?"

"Why should she want to hurt a stray?" Chad asked angrily. "What's that got to do with anything?"

"Oh, I don't know. A cat that's wild might be vicious or maybe diseased or—I don't know, Chad. But I'll talk to her. That's the way to find out."

"No," Chad said. "I can fight my own battles.

Thanks anyway . . . Maybe I'll go talk to her again myself."

"I'll go with you," Polly offered.

"Okay," Chad said. If he had Polly with him, he wouldn't be as apt to lose his temper with Mrs. Saugerty, and maybe with Polly, the old lady would act nice. "Let's go get it over with now."

He led the way over the hill, carefully skirting the poison ivy patch that had not given him any trouble but to which Polly might be allergic. Mrs. Saugerty's car was not parked in her driveway.

"She's probably out doing some last minute shopping," Polly said. "There's always last minute shopping when company's due."

"You want to wait a while or come back later?" Chad asked.

"Let's wait." Polly sat down on the steps to the front door and Chad sat next to her, though he would have chosen to stay out of sight at the edge of the woods. The gray Persian was sitting on a cushion inside the living-room window among the potted plants, watching them through half-closed eyes.

"Doesn't she let her cat out?" Polly asked.

"Sometimes. Most of the time she keeps him inside."

"I wonder if he minds."

"Why should he mind? She feeds him plenty, probably better food than a lot of humans get. He's warm and comfortable and nobody's after him with a shotgun like my cat in the dump."

"But he doesn't have any freedom."

Chad thought about his cat roaming around, investigating the world, sniffing the breeze on the beach, playing with the early morning shadows in the woods, prancing down to the pier to see what was up. It was a pretty good life from that point of view. "I guess being cooped up with an old lady like Mrs. Saugerty can't be much fun," Chad observed.

They watched the chickadees, with wings outstretched and feathers absurdly puffed, dip themselves into the birdbath, then hop back to the rim and shake the water off.

"When I leave with my mom, I'm going to take the cat with me," Chad said.

"But Chad—"

"What?"

"Have you heard from your mother yet?"

"Not yet."

"I asked my mother about—about what you told me about your mother—"

He was furious. "You told your mother what I told you?"

"I didn't know I shouldn't! What are you so mad about?"

"When I tell you something, it's not to blab to the world about. And what do you mean? You asked her what? What does your mother know anyway?"

"But Chad, my mother says—"

"I don't care what your mother says. She doesn't know my mother. I told you—every time she visited me, no matter where I was, my mother always said she was going to take me to live with her, and now I'm old enough, *now* is the time."

He felt hot and jumpy, and the look of disbelief on Polly's face made him hate her. "What do you know about my mother anyway?" he said. "Why don't you go home? I don't need you here. You're just a fat, stupid girl." He would have hit her except that she was a girl and staring at him with her innocent blue eyes. All of a sudden she got up and fled from him.

"Go stick your head in a book where you belong," he yelled after her.

Chad was alone when the car pulled in the driveway, and Mrs. Saugerty heaved her bulk out of the driver's seat. "Chad! I'm glad you're here," the old lady said, not noticing his black mood. "You can help me in with my bundles. I bought out the supermarket. Didn't realize all I had until the checkout girl started bagging it. I told her to put it in small parcels, but she was a snippy little thing—said the store's policy wouldn't allow it. Here now, I'll unlock the door and you start unloading."

"I'm not helping you with anything until you promise me something."

"Promise you what?"

"That you won't put out rat poison to kill my cat—not rat poison or any other kind of stuff that'll hurt him."

"Why should I promise you that?"

"Because I won't help you ever again if you don't."

Mrs. Saugerty's face went red. "What gives you the notion I need your help? I thought I was doing you a favor paying you for yard work. I can just as easy hire someone else. Plenty of strong young boys looking for work during the summer, and much nicer ones than you, too, ones that know how to keep a civil tongue in their head. The trouble with you is you've got no manners."

Chad stared at her, overcome with the hopelessness of winning her sympathy. Why should she do anything for him? Probably she could see how much he hated her.

He turned and fled back over the hill feeling sick to his stomach. He had made an awful mess of it. It was worse than before. First he had turned on Polly and been mean to her, and now he had made Mrs. Saugerty so mad she would probably kill his cat just for spite. Why did he have such a rotten temper? So far it had cost him two perfectly nice foster homes. Both times he'd been kicked out when he lost control of his temper.

The first time he'd smashed a kid who called Chad's mother something nasty through a glass cold frame where tomato plants were growing. The kid swore Chad had attacked him without reason, and the kid's friend backed him in the lie.

The second time was worse. That foster father was in a wheelchair and they had a retarded daughter and a son who was jealous because his mother favored Chad. Chad really liked that lady. She was big and fat and she laughed a lot. She was helping support her family by taking care of three or four foster children besides all she had to take care of with her husband and her daughter.

Chad had tried to help as much as an eleven-year-old could who wasn't all that big. The lady's mistake was to say to her son how he should be more like Chad. Next thing Chad knew he was accused of doing something bad to the retarded girl. He went wild then and got after the brother with a piece of stove wood.

The caseworker he had then had warned him, "You'll end up in jail, Chad Thomas Lester." He did not want to end up in jail. But no matter how he tried to hold himself in when he got mad, eventually a point would come when he exploded without even giving himself enough warning so he could run somewhere to cool off.

He halted at the kitchen door to the Sorenics' cottage, breathing hard and feeling miserable. How was he going to face Polly? Suppose she had told her mother! Now he was going to be in for it.

Chad heard the sounds of dishes clicking against one another and the refrigerator door opening in the kitchen. He waited, eavesdropping on Polly and her mother.

"Mom, there's a cooked hamburger in here still that Bob said he was going to eat."

"Put it out for lunch. If nobody wants it, Chad can give it to the cat. Where is he incidentally?"

"Still waiting to talk to Mrs. Saugerty probably."

"I hope he gets back soon. We have to make the Truro parking lot by one o'clock for that guided dunes walk we're taking. We ought to leave here about twelve-thirty."

Chad guessed by the tone of the conversation that Polly had not said anything. He felt guilty. She was such a neat girl, and he was so rotten. He opened the screen door and stepped into the kitchen.

"Polly, I'm sorry," he said. "I didn't mean a word I said to you."

"I know," Polly said.

Pam looked at them inquiringly. "Have a fight, you two?"

"It wasn't anything," Polly said. She looked at Chad with concern. "Did you talk to Mrs. Saugerty?"

"I blew it. I think I made things worse." Chad looked down and discovered the pattern of red bricks in the floor covering.

"Everybody blows it sometime or other," Pam said. He felt her arms go around him and the quick hug. She had never touched him before though she often hugged or kissed her own kids. "Buck up, Chad. It can't be nearly as bad as it seems." Pam's sympathy broke Chad down entirely. He made a run for the bedroom and rolled into a ball on his bunk.

Chapter 9

In the car on the way to Truro, Pam told Roger about the problem of Mrs. Saugerty and the rat poison. Roger said, "Maybe the best thing to do is to keep the cat locked up in the cottage for a while, Chad."

"He's not used to being indoors. He might wreck the place."

"You could keep him in your bedroom if you're careful—you and Bob. Not much he can destroy in there, is there?"

"My tennis racquet," Bob said.

"Stow that in the living room," Roger suggested.

"Well, I'd appreciate it," Chad said, "if Bob doesn't mind having the cat around—I mean, it's his room and—"

"So long as he doesn't mess on my bed, I don't mind."

"I'll get some kitty litter and a pan from the

supermarket," Pam offered. "You can fill a box with sand till then."

"He might not know enough to use it," Chad warned, still wallowing in his gloom.

"Ah, come on, Chad. Don't make more problems than you've got already," Bob replied.

There was another problem Chad thought of, but decided not to mention. How long did they have to keep the cat locked in for safety's sake? The rat poison would keep and could be put out again in a week or two or four. The cat was used to being free. He couldn't be kept inside indefinitely.

"You know," Pam said, "it's possible that the cat was in somebody's house when he was a kitten. Maybe he'll take to being indoors easier than you think, Chad."

They were all so nice. Chad couldn't believe how nice they were. He had lived with people who were nice before, but never where everybody went out of their way to help Chad Thomas Lester particularly.

Later that day, after the dunes walk, Chad was under the pine tree waiting for the cat to come by toward evening as it had taken to doing. Bob appeared beside him, dressed in cutoffs, swinging his tennis racquet, ready for his late afternoon practice session. Chad tensed, thinking Bob had decided he didn't want the cat kept in their bedroom after all.

"Listen," Bob said. "I was thinking about that rat poison."

"Yeah?"

"That old lady—where does she keep stuff like insect sprays and dusting powders, stuff like that?"

"In her garage."

"So where's she going to store that rat poison?"

Chad thought about it. The garage was possible, a safer spot than kitchen or bathroom for something poisonous. "Maybe in the garage."

"And does she ever leave it open when she goes out?"

"I've never seen her close the garage door, not even when she's home. She leaves it open all the time."

"So it would be easy to grab the stuff out of the garage and get rid of it before she uses it, wouldn't it?"

"You mean steal it? But she'd know it was me who took it. I mean, who else is gonna steal rat poison from her?"

"Yeah, I guess. Well, it was just an idea." Bob twirled the tennis racquet and turned to leave. Chad was about to thank him for trying when an idea hit him.

"Hey, Bob. Suppose we took the stuff and emptied it out and put in something safe that looked the same—like flour or sugar or whatever. I mean, like if the container is a box, something we could close and make it look like it was never opened."

"Yeah, that's possible. Then what do we do with the poison? You can't just throw that stuff in the bay, you know. It'll pollute everything."

"We can bury it, like atomic wastes! Or we could put it in a plastic bag and seal it good and take it to the dump or something."

Bob nodded. "I'll help you if you want me to. So long as it doesn't interfere with my practice."

"Thanks, Bob. I mean I really appreciate . . . thanks."

In all the weeks he and Bob had shared a room, Chad had never said more to him than, "These your socks under the bed?" or "Mind if I close the windows?" And twice now Bob had proven himself to be a decent guy. Chad was ashamed of himself for labeling him "jock" and then ignoring him.

"See you later," Bob said and ambled off swinging his racquet. Of course, there was still the guy in the dump even if they did get rid of the rat poison. But you could not worry about everything. After all, the cat could get hit by a car as it crossed a road. Some things had to be left to chance.

The cat padded out of the underbrush and kept coming straight toward Chad, its pupils trusting black seeds in the centers of its yellow eyes. It plunked itself down on Chad's lap, wrapping its tail around itself as neatly as if it were sitting down on an ice cream stool. Chad chuckled and stroked the cat firmly from head to tail, then scratched around its ears. A ragged purr began in the cat's throat. "I didn't think you could purr, Cat," Chad said. He wondered if this was the first time it ever had.

"Hey Cat, my cat," Chad whispered. The cat leaned its head against Chad's cheek with its eyes closed and its whiskers tickling as it purred contentedly.

All the way back to the cottage, the cat lay relaxed in Chad's arms, but when Chad opened the kitchen door with one free hand, it tensed. Its head came up alertly and it let out a feeble cry, its body gathering itself to jump. Chad spoke soothingly but held on as the cat dug in its claws. Even against the pain of the claws, Chad held on all the way into the bedroom. "Don't be afraid now. Nobody's going to hurt you. This is all for your own good," Chad murmured. But when he got the door shut and released the cat, it streaked around the room in a frenzy—under the dresser, under the chair, to the top of the bunk beds, back under the dresser. There it crouched, staring out, its eyes now black with terror.

Chad sat down on the bed to wait for the cat to calm down, but it stayed hidden under the dresser.

"Chad?"

It was Polly's voice. "Don't come in. The cat's in here," Chad warned.

"We're going to the beach. You coming?"

Eventually the cat would make peace with its new surroundings, but Chad didn't see much point in waiting around for that to happen.

"Yeah, I'm coming." He put on the cutoffs he used for swimming and eased himself out the door, barely opening it as he did. The cat had not budged.

Chapter 10

I n the mornings that followed, Chad would wake up to find the cat nestled into the crook of his legs, but once out of bed, Chad and everyone else had to be on constant alert to keep the cat in the house. It would hide under the couch in the living room and streak for the door as soon as anyone opened it. In the kitchen its favorite spot was the top of the refrigerator. From there it would watch the family as they ate, every once in a while letting out a pitiful yowl. Alone with Chad, the cat would walk to the nearest door and cry, open-mouthed, pleading to be released.

"It's for your own good," Chad would tell it over and over, explaining about the poison and Mrs. Saugerty as if the cat could understand.

"Now you know how a parent feels when he's got to say 'no' to his kid," Roger told Chad.

"I wish I could just let him out."

94

"Sure, it's hard making somebody do something they don't like for their own good."

"Yeah, I see what you mean." Chad figured a week would have to do it. That was how long Mrs. Saugerty's guests were supposed to stay. He counted the days and was grateful that the Sorenics were all careful about where the cat was when they entered or left the cottage. The cat had started using the litter pan the first day, but otherwise it remained untamed, keeping its distance from everyone in the family except Polly, whom it allowed to approach and pet it. The only one the cat itself chose to go to was Chad.

Thursday the sky was thick gray and the water flat mean. Bob was sleeping late. The rest of the family had taken a jaunt down to Provincetown for the day. Chad left the cat in his bedroom and hiked down to the pier. Nobody but old Chester was fishing. He was a lumpy figure in his old seaman's cap and shapeless jacket, looking as gray and spiritless as the day.

"Catch anything?" Chad asked in greeting.

The old man peered at him. "Haven't seen you for a week. Didn't expect you *this* morning."

"It's rotten weather, isn't it? I mean for summer."

"Mean, cold, and cantankerous like an old man living alone."

Chester sounded depressed. Chad wondered if it was just the weather or if something else was wrong.

"How come you don't stay home by your stove on a day like today, Chester?"

"Get enough of that all winter. I brought a thermos of hot coffee. Want some?"

"No thanks."

"Bring the fishing gear I got you?"

Chad held up the gray string line on the bleached wood shuttle and the paper bag in which he had a card of hooks, several different-sized sinkers and a box of worms. He had spent his last earnings from Mrs. Saugerty on the worms. The day that Chester had given him the gear, Chad had pulled up three flounder, causing the old man to grin and say he was a natural-born fisherman. But when Chad brought the flounder proudly home, the fish had looked insignificant cut up and frying in the pan for lunch, only a mouthful for each of them. Privately Chad had decided fishing was a dumb sport.

"Bought us both some bait." Chad opened the box and surveyed the plump reddish-colored worms.

"Careful they don't bite the ends of your finger off when you string them on the hook. Know how?"

Chester showed him. Chad was amazed that worms could bite. "You can keep them in the refrigerator if you don't use them up today," Chester said. "You warm enough in that thin jacket?"

"Sure," Chad said. He was glad he had come. The old man seemed to have cheered up.

"Yep," Chester said, settling back to his fishing. "Missed you. Your cat hasn't been by neither."

"I've got him locked in the cottage. The lady in the house behind us is trying to poison him."

"You don't say? He sure has got himself a lot of enemies for a young feller, don't he?"

"I guess so."

"What'll happen to him at the end of the summer when you leave?"

"I'll take him with me. My mom won't mind."

"You're going home to your mom?"

"I hope so."

"Hope so, huh? It's better not to hope for too much in this world. Then you don't get disappointed. Less hope you got, the better off you are."

"But if you can't hope for anything good, what's the use of living?" Chad argued against the old man's glum philosophy.

"Oh, a young feller like you can hope. Why not? You got a long ways to go before you can stop wanting things or depending on people."

"I don't depend on anybody but myself," Chad said proudly.

"Well, that's good. Course you're a little young to be on your own. What about your mother? Aren't you depending on her?"

Chad did not answer immediately. He could feel himself getting agitated at the old man's questions.

He *was* cranky this morning, the old man was. Of course, Chad knew better than to think he could depend on his mother. But if she didn't agree to the proposal in his letter, then what would he do? Run away alone? He couldn't take the cat even if he did, and he didn't want to run away. Dependency—Mrs. Saugerty had said something about it too. Mean old lady. Chad remembered her triumphant voice, "It's only yours if it can depend on you." She'd said that about the cat. Chad felt the line tug and jerked it viciously.

"Gonna lose your fish that way," Chester said.

Chad rolled his line around the shuttle reeling in. Sure enough his hook was bare. He set the box of worms down next to Chester. "I don't feel much like fishing today anyway, Chester. It's too cold."

"I got a sweater in the truck you could use."

Chad fidgeted. "No thanks." He could tolerate the chill. He just didn't feel like talking to Chester anymore.

"I was thinking this morning," Chester mused, "about how after my wife died, my daughter and me depended on each other. Course she needed me to feed and clothe her, but I needed her too. You have someone you care for, that makes it worthwhile. Then she grew up and got married and moved away. I never told her, but it was awful hard for me living alone. Course I went a long ways on habit. And I got used to it. Now I wouldn't give up my independence, not if someone offered me the coziest berth with a cup of hot tea delivered to my bedside every morning ... that's when it's hardest, the mornings—the getting up for nothing..." His rambling voice trailed off foghorn-lonely, and Chad waited, unwilling to just walk off and leave him there.

"Course nights in the winter is hard too, but it's a good thing to find you don't need nobody but your own self."

"Your daughter write you that she can't come?" Chad guessed out loud.

"How did you know? Did I tell you? ... Yeah, she had to use the money for the kids' teeth. Said maybe next summer." He reeled in and flipped a dinner-plate-sized flounder up on the dock. "Now there's a nice one," he said dolefully.

"Yeah," Chad said. He threaded another section of sand worm on his hook. The least he could do was keep Chester company today.

Three hours of fishing produced a plastic bag full of flounder which Chad carried back to the cottage. The weather had lifted, and the gray cracked open to let broad shafts of sunlight through, warm on Chad's back as he jogged down the harbor beach. He had been gone a long time. As he neared the cottage, he began worrying about how the cat had done inside alone with Bob. He had no sooner entered the kitchen than he found out.

"Chad?" Bob called.

"Yeah, it's me."

"Your cat got out. I was just taking the garbage out, and I thought he was still in the bedroom. He ran right between my feet."

The whole pit of Chad's stomach fell away. "You dumb jerk!" Chad snapped. He tore up to the pine tree and waited there, calling and whistling every so often, but no cat appeared. Then he ran down to the harbor beach and back down to the marina. Chester had already left and nobody Chad asked had seen a black-and-white cat. He ran back up the road to the cottage. Last of all, with sinking heart, he snuck down to Mrs. Saugerty's.

Two cars parked behind hers in the driveway and the sound of country western music coming from the house told him her guests were still around. Chad skulked around the edges of the lawn, but he didn't see any poisoned bait. Maybe she wouldn't put any out until her company left. If she thought about it, her cat could get outside just like his had, and then *it* might take the bait. No, she wouldn't take a chance on poisoning her own cat. Chad had not thought of that before. It calmed him down. He returned to the cottage and found Bob reading the old pile of comic books in the living room.

"Bob, I'm sorry I yelled at you. I know you didn't mean to let the cat out."

"No, I didn't," Bob said. He looked at Chad coldly, still hurt.

Later, when the rest of the family got back from Provincetown with a box of saltwater taffy for the stay-at-homes, Chad told Polly his reasoning about the cat.

"I'm sure you're right," Polly said. "We've probably been keeping him locked in the cottage all week for nothing."

They were playing checkers. Chad jumped her king with his. He was good at checkers. Polly sighed, exasperated at losing again, and asked, "When are you going to name him anyway?"

"Name who?"

"The cat. He ought to have a name, don't you think?"

Chad thought about it. "If I give him a name, that means like—he's dependent on me or something."

"And you don't want him to be?"

"The thing is—I don't know if I can keep him." Suppose his mother didn't come through? The Children's Shelter didn't allow pets. Most foster families wouldn't let him keep a pet either. "Maybe he's better off just 'Cat,' " Chad said. He sounded as doleful as Chester.

Chapter 11

"Chad," Pam said at lunchtime that Saturday when they were all sitting around the kitchen table, "I saw Mrs. Saugerty's guests driving off in fully packed cars this morning. Where's your cat?"

"He came for his breakfast and then took off down toward the marina."

"Well, now that she's alone again, I think I'll go have a talk with her," Pam said.

"You mean, see about the poison?"

"I mean, maybe I can put some social pressure on her to keep her from using it."

"I don't know what you mean." Chad didn't see Mrs. Saugerty being talked out of anything she wanted to do, and besides he still had Bob's plan to try. "Look," he said. "Don't you bother about my cat. I'll take care of him."

"How?"

"Don't worry. I won't get into any trouble."

"Probably Mrs. Saugerty was just talking anyway," Pam said. "She probably has no intention of setting out poisoned bait."

Chad disagreed. Pam could say something like that because she was too nice herself to imagine anyone being mean enough to poison a cat. Mrs. Saugerty was mean enough.

Chad was starting up the hill alone when he heard Bob hail him. Ever since Chad called him a jerk for letting the cat out, Bob had avoided talking to him. Now Bob came up the hill and asked, "You going to steal the poison now?"

"Going to try."

"I'll go with you if you want."

"That'd be good. You could be lookout for me."

Bob nodded, his square, fleshy face expressionless.

"Let's go see if she's home," Chad said.

They walked over the hill together not saying much, but Chad was glad Bob had gotten over his anger, glad of his companionship. They stopped at the edge of Mrs. Saugerty's property and hid behind a high bush loaded with fat cones of white clustered flowerets.

"The garage is open," Bob whispered.

"Always is. Her car's here though, so she must be too. Don't see her in the living room. Don't see her big cat either. She could be in the kitchen or lying down. If she's taking a nap, I could sneak into the garage and look for it."

"Where do you want me to stay?"

"Stay here. Then if I'm in the garage and she comes out, you could start talking to her about something and give me time to get away."

"Talking about what?"

"I don't know. Ask her if she wants a boy to cut the lawn or something."

"How about if I go into the garage and you be lookout?" Bob said.

"Why?"

"You're the talker. I won't know what to say to her."

Chad considered. He couldn't really imagine Bob keeping Mrs. Saugerty occupied for very long. Conversation squeezed out of Bob like toothpaste from an empty tube. And it was true Chad could keep the old lady talking forever. All he had to do was accuse her of short changing him or something, and she'd be too distracted to even look toward the garage.

"Yeah, okay," Chad said. "I'll wait here. If she comes out, I'll talk loud, and you circle back around the way you came. Keep your head down. Hug the house so she can't look out the window and see you, and circle around the back. The only bad spot will be the kitchen door. If she's in the kitchen, she could see you as you go past the door. If she comes out

104

then—." He thought a minute. "We'll just say we lost a—a—ball or something—no, an arrow."

"But we don't have any bows."

"A kite maybe."

Bob shrugged. "Okay."

"Now when you get the stuff—box or bag or whatever it's in—you empty it into this plastic bag and then fill it back up with this sack of sugar. Then shove the box back on the shelf or wherever you found it and come back the way you came."

"Got you."

Chad didn't like it. He would rather be doing this part himself, but he slapped Bob on the shoulder as if he had full confidence in the younger boy's ability. The kid took the two bags and set off, head down, running for the house, looking suspicious already. If Chad were doing the job himself, and Mrs. Saugerty caught him, he could lie his way out handily. With Bob doing it, the whole operation was more chancy. Suppose he knocked over one of the shelves bulging with stuff that lined the garage walls, so that only a very small car could fit between them?

Chad chewed his lip thinking about all those neatly labeled packing boxes. It would take forever for Bob even to locate the poison. He should never have let the kid take over. But Bob wanted to help, and Chad hadn't wanted to hurt his feelings.

Chad picked up a twig to chew on instead of his lip

———

105

which was getting sore from the mauling he had been giving it. By now Bob had to be in the garage. Where was Mrs. Saugerty? Napping if they were lucky. She *could* be napping. She must be tired after all that company.

The screen door opened. Mrs. Saugerty stepped out onto the stoop and looked around. Then she had heard something! "Freeze," Chad told Bob inside his head. "Freeze." If she came down the steps to investigate, Chad would pretend to be just coming out of the woods. He'd yell, "Mrs. Saugerty, can I see you for a minute?" He had the words ready on his tongue but she turned back into the house, locking the screen door behind her.

Waiting was bad as an itch you couldn't scratch. Chad had no watch but he guessed Bob had started off close to an hour ago. What was the kid doing? Suppose he had found the rat poison and headed home already, circling around the woods in back of the hill where Chad couldn't see him, leaving Chad here to wait and worry for nothing. All because he hadn't thought to tell Bob to signal him when the job was done and it was okay to leave. How long should he stay crouched here with his legs aching? A bee buzzed his nose. Chad shooed him off.

No, Bob was supposed to come back here, Chad thought. That had been the plan. Unless he'd forgotten. Chad strained to hear what was going on, but all he heard was the steady drone of the insects interrupted by a trill, varied by a whistle, accompanied by the wind rustling through the leaves. He was perspiring from nervousness. He would watch the sun, he thought. As soon as it moved in line with a naked twig sticking up from Mrs. Saugerty's shade tree, Chad would sneak around the house himself and see what was happening.

He blinked twice when he saw the car marked SHERIFF swing into the driveway and stop. A gray-haired man in a short-sleeved white shirt and gray pants jumped out; ordering, "Okay. Come on out of there and start explaining yourself!"

Bob stepped out of the garage and just stood there. The front door popped open again. Mrs. Saugerty hauled herself down the steps in a hurry to put in her two cents.

"Who are you?" she asked Bob. "I heard something in the garage and called the police. Last time it was a raccoon, but you never can tell. What are you looking to steal in there, boy?"

"Nothing," Bob said.

He could have said he was after his cat, Chad thought. He could have said his cat went into the garage and he just . . . Bob was going to get in trouble. The Sheriff would take him in and they'd call the Sorenics. Why didn't the dumb kid admit he was just helping Chad out? Bob didn't want to steal anything for himself. Why didn't he defend himself? Chad couldn't stand it. He stood up. No point letting it go further. He could not let Bob take the rap alone.

Nobody noticed Chad until he stopped right next to Mrs. Saugerty. "What are you doing here?" she asked.

"I came to get the rat poison. I sent Bob in to get it while I was lookout."

"What's that? Who are you?" the Sheriff wanted to know.

"I'm Chad Thomas Lester—" Chad began, but Mrs. Saugerty interrupted.

"He's my yard boy. Lives over the hill with the Sorenics." She turned to Chad. "What's this about rat poison?"

"I sent Bob in to get it for me so you couldn't kill my cat like you said."

"I *never* said I was going to kill any cat," Mrs. Saugerty protested. "What a terrible thing to accuse me of. You should know me better than to think I'd go around poisoning cats, Chad."

"But you said—"

"I never said any such thing. If I mentioned rat poison to you at all, it was to rid my basement of the vermin that gets in there when the cool weather comes. I keep hearing noises down there at night, and last year when I stored a bushel of apples—"

"Mrs. Saugerty," the Sheriff interrupted. "You want me to take these youngsters down and book them or what?"

"I don't know."

"Bob didn't take anything," Chad said.

"I couldn't find it," Bob spoke up.

"What?" the Sheriff asked.

"The rat poison."

"There isn't any," Mrs. Saugerty said. "My son forgot to bring it. I have it on my list of things to get in the city. Around here nobody . . ."

"Well, do you want me to book them or not?"

"It grieves me," Mrs. Saugerty said to Chad, ignoring the impatient Sheriff. "It just grieves me to know you'd think me as mean as all that."

"You're not going to kill my cat?"

"Certainly not. Of course, if he gets mangy or diseased, I might get someone to put him out of his misery. That I might do."

"Okay. Well, I'm sorry then," Chad said.

"You'd better be. I'm really disappointed in you."

"So are we going to charge the kids or not?" the Sheriff demanded wearily.

"I don't think so. Not this time," Mrs. Saugerty said. "You're not going to come prowling around my house again, are you, young man?" She turned to Bob.

"No, ma'am," Bob said politely.

Chad shuffled his feet. The Sheriff sighed. "All right, Mrs. Saugerty. I guess that's it then. Be seeing you."

"Well," Mrs. Saugerty said, after the sheriff had gone, "aren't you ashamed of yourself trying to make me look bad like that?"

"You *did* say you wanted to get rid of my cat."

"And if I said it? That doesn't mean I'd go so far as to do anything—certainly not with rat poison my own cat could get at."

"Oh!" Chad said.

"What do you mean, 'Oh'? I don't like your attitude, young man. If you want to work for me anymore, you better just apologize."

"For what?" Chad said. "You would of done it if you hadn't been scared that Lord Elgin might be the one to get killed."

"Fresh! You're just a fresh-mouthed boy, and I'm not saying another word to you until *you* say you're sorry." She turned and stumped angrily back into her house, snapping the screen door shut behind her.

Climbing back over the hill, Chad said, "Boy, was that dumb! That was really stupid."

"What was?"

"The whole thing. I'm sorry I got you into it, Bob."

"Oh, I don't know."

"You don't know what?"

110

"It was exciting, sort of. It was good you stood up for me though. I wouldn't of liked it if the sheriff had called my dad."

"Yeah, I wouldn't of liked it either."

"Well, if you ever need my help again—"

"I can count on you?"

"Yeah."

"You can count on me too," Chad said. "Put're there!" He held his hand out. Bob shook it. The kid was all right, Chad thought with a slow pleasure.

Chapter 12

Chad would have enjoyed the last weeks of the summer if he could have shaken off the nagging worry about the letter from his mother he kept expecting every day, but which did not come. With the cat off his private endangered species list, it was hard not to think about himself. So much depended on that letter. Chad didn't expect the Sorenics to keep him past the summer. After all, they hadn't even wanted a boy in the first place. So if his mother didn't agree to make a home with him, there would be another placement, another family, another town, another school.

Most of the time though, Chad was having too much fun to brood. He had become as much of a beach lover, both ocean and bay sides, as the Sorenics. He liked horsing around with Bob and having long, thoughtful conversations with Polly. There was Chester and the fishing and playing with the cat. Even the carpentry work Roger had finally gotten Chad involved in was satisfying. Roger had explained the overall project, then taught Chad and Bob about the measuring and cutting and how to do the joining. Chad figured carpentry was a good skill to have and, besides, he was good at it, according to Roger.

The morning the letter came, Chad was working on bookshelves. Roger had explained what he had to do and then left him alone to do it. That was how Chad liked to work. He hated just handing out nails and holding things steady for somebody else.

"Between this and the rain, I haven't had any tennis practice for two days," Bob complained.

Chad ran his fingers over the wood he was sanding, feeling for the rough spots, and listening.

"I know, fella," Roger answered his son, "but I hate to stop in the middle of a job. Soon as we finish, you can get in all the practice you want."

"If it doesn't rain again," Bob said, sawing with sudden spurts of energy and a lot of perspiration.

"Who's got the level?" Roger asked.

"Here it is." Chad handed it to him.

"Neat job," Roger said, checking out the two shelves Chad had finished. "You learn amazingly fast."

"I like working with my hands." Chad liked the

smell of the freshly cut wood, too, and the way the grain made patterns of light and dark.

"If you like to work with your hands," Pam called from the bedroom where she and Polly were antiquing a chest of drawers, "I could teach you how to knit."

"I wouldn't mind," Chad said as if she weren't teasing.

"He likes to cook too," Polly said. "You ought to let him make a pie for us sometime, Mom. He says his crusts are super."

"Oh boy!" Bob groaned. "If that isn't sick!"

"Why?" Roger asked.

"Chad's no girl."

"Most chefs are men," Roger pointed out. "And I wouldn't risk sounding like a male chauvinist around here, Bob."

"Bob was born a male chauvinist," Polly said. "It came with his blue blanket."

"Well, guys are stronger. That's the truth," Bob said.

"Girls are probably more agile though," Roger suggested.

"And girls are smarter," Chad put in.

"Do you think so, Chad?" Pam called. "There, Polly! I always thought Chad was an exceptionally perceptive young man. There's the proof."

"Well, I wouldn't go that far to say girls are smarter," Roger said.

The conversation ran back and forth, light as a Ping-Pong ball, in between the painting and sawing and hammering. Finally Bob said, "Okay. Dad, I'm calling it quits for today. I've done my share."

"How come you're so conscientious about tennis and not about anything else?" Roger asked.

"That's not fair."

"Isn't it? Look at the mess you've made there. You've got one board cut two inches shorter than the other. Your mind's on winning tennis matches instead of on what you're supposed to be doing."

Bob frowned. "If that's the way you feel, then you don't need me here." He slammed into his bedroom and came out, head down, face flushed with anger, and with his racquet and balls clenched in his hands.

"Your big problem still is you can't take criticism," Roger said to his son's departing back.

"Bob's a good kid. He just doesn't like carpentry work," Chad said. "He does a lot of other things around here."

"Bob's okay. He's got some growing up to do that's all. What do you say, Chad? Shall we varnish these shelves or paint them?"

"Varnish. That way the grain will show."

"I agree with Chad," Pam called from the bedroom.

"The women in this family always agree with Chad," Roger replied. "However, this time I have to admit I agree myself. Of course, that means we'll have to stop work while I go into town and buy some varnish."

Chad spied the cat waiting for him up at the pine tree when he went into the kitchen to wash up. "I'll grab a sandwich later," he told Pam, then climbed the hill to sit under the pine and pet the cat. The cat stretched into ridiculous positions in Chad's arms, purring with gusto as Chad stroked its belly and under its chin. They were still playing in the patched sun and shadow when Polly walked up the hill with a white envelope in her hand.

"A letter came for you. Dad brought the mail back with him." Polly held out the envelope. Concern made her freckled face look older than it was. "It looks like it's from your mother."

Chad saw the sympathy darkening Polly's blue eyes and was scared. "Thanks," he said. He took the letter and held it at his side until she left. The cat stalked off unnoticed.

When Chad finally looked down at the envelope, a memory flashed in his head: His mother running toward him, young, pretty, her long wavy hair streaming out behind her. She caught him up in her arms and kissed him all over his face, "My baby, my own, my sweet little darling . . ." Chad couldn't remember the foster parents he had had then; he must have been very small, but he remembered another kid saying to him enviously, "Gee, your mother sure loves you." It had kept him going then to know that his mother loved him, but he was afraid now.

He ran to the cottage and through to his room without looking at anyone. With the door closed behind him, he lay down on his bunk, squeezing the unopened letter in his hands.

Once there had been a Ferris wheel. He must have been seven or eight. A man came with her that time, and it was in his car they had driven to the amusement park. "Is he my daddy?" Chad had whispered in his mother's ear.

"No, honey, but I wish he was," and she had giggled like a kid.

On the Ferris wheel, she had sat between him and the man. She had squealed as if she were afraid, and Chad had said, "Don't be scared, Mama. I'm with you."

She had laughed and said to the man proudly, "Isn't he something?" But that too had happened a long time ago. Nothing recent had been half so nice.

Gingerly, Chad opened the envelope. The letter was short, just half a sheet of notepaper.

Dear Chad,

Well, I am now a Mrs. He kept his promise and married me proper in the church and we have a little house and his dog which sleeps on the bed with us but otherwise is no bother. So I am doing O.K. Thank you for the ten dollars. I am sorry I can't send you nothing right now, but you know how things are right at the beginning.

Now Chad I have to tell you I am really sorry about the adoption. I never wanted to give you up. I love you and tried hard to keep you as you are my own dear son but how things work out is up to the Lord so you mustnt blame your Mama too much. I mean the best for you always. But now it is out of my hands and though I will miss seeing you, I know the Lord will provide for you as he does for me. You be a good boy and don't be mad at me if I don't send you my new address. Like I told you before my husband don't want me to have nothing to do with you now and maybe it is all for the best for both of us.

~~Your loving mother~~
Love and kisses,
April Anne

Chad was stunned. The letter hurt him, but the closing was what he could not bear. She had crossed out "Your loving mother" and substituted something neutral, as if she were practicing not being his mother. She had disowned him for that man. He had no mother anymore. In a cold sweat he read the letter through one more time; then he tore it into little pieces and threw them. He threw them up and screamed at the top of his lungs, and when that was not enough, he lurched off his bed and hurled the straight-backed chair he and Bob used to hang their clothes on at night at the dresser. The mirror shattered with a fine, loud crash. That sobered him some.

He dashed out of the house, back up the hill, and crashed through the underbrush until he found a tree with branches trailing to the ground. He rolled under the branches and began banging his head against the trunk of the tree, banging doggedly until the physical hurt overlaid the other. The blood dripping down his forehead into his eye stopped him. He curled into a ball and lay there just barely able to endure, waiting for whatever came next.

Sometime later he felt a hand on his shoulder. He looked around and saw Polly squatting awkwardly behind him in the limited space under the pine tree.

"Chad, are you all right?"

"No."

"Oh. You hurt yourself! Oh, Chad, she said she can't take you?"

"Yeah."

"Well, you aren't going to just lie up here until you die, are you?"

"Maybe."

"Come on. It's almost time for dinner. Mom wants you to come back. She's been fussing all afternoon making you cookies and stuff like you were sick."

Chad saw through the pine needles that the light had changed. Now it was the color of weak tea, late afternoon. "Polly, I don't think I can come back to the cottage."

"Sure you can. Why not?"

He sat up. His head throbbed horribly, and he saw Polly grimace at his forehead. "My mother's not my mother anymore. She's through with me."

Polly took his hand and squeezed it. "You've got us."

He shook his head. "No, you're not my family."

"Well, we could be maybe."

"Polly, you're a good kid, but you don't know much. I don't have nobody now. I don't belong nowhere."

"You still have the cat."

"No. I can't take him with me now. I'm going to have to leave him behind just like the people did last year." He started to quiver, hid his face against his knees.

"At least come on in and wash the blood off you," she said.

He took a deep breath. His throat was raw, and he felt nauseous. "Okay, you go ahead. I'll come."

It was already dark under the trees on their side of

the hill. The kitchen window glowed like a square sun; the cottage looked inviting. Chad walked through it to the bathroom without looking at anyone. He washed his face against the stinging of his forehead and dabbed on some of the antiseptic Pam had in the medicine cabinet. He looked like an accident victim, pale, drawn face and bloodied forehead. He combed his hair forward to hide the worst of it and slunk back to the kitchen. Pam was the only one there.

"How about a cup of tea?" she asked.

"I'm sorry about the room," he said.

"Tell me about the letter, Chad."

He stiffened. It was none of her business. Nobody's business but his, and he didn't want to talk about it. Then he looked up at Pam, sitting across the table from him with tea ready and milk if he wanted it and a plate of cookies baked just for him. Pam's saucer eyes shone with sympathy. Chad's defenses collapsed. "She married some guy in a church," he muttered. "Now she doesn't want me anymore. She says she's not my mother now. I'm too old."

When he shuddered, Pam came around the table and held him close against the warmth of her body. The comfort of her arms made him begin to cry.

"I'm sure she hasn't stopped loving you, Chad. Nobody could. You're too fine a boy for her not to care about you . . . It's probably just that she's had it rough for so long that she couldn't refuse when that man offered to marry her. She had to save herself so she let you go, but I'm sure she still loves you, Chad."

Pam's arms stayed around him and the soothing murmur of her sympathy. "Once," he began, but had to gulp before he could go on. "Once she told me there wasn't anybody closer to her in the world than me." He remembered that visit so well. It was a rainy day, and the house he was staying in then had three or four babies all down with colds and crying. Their crying got on his mother's nerves, so they had gone for a walk in the rain. It was so nice to be alone with her, even though she wasn't laughing and affectionate as she usually was. She was sad, and she said that to him when they were standing under a tree near some swings. "There isn't anybody closer to me in this world than you, Chad." He felt proud when she said that. He felt like . . . "But it was a lie, Pam," Chad now said out loud. "She was just lying to me."

"No," Pam replied. "She wasn't lying. It's just that you're still a child and she's not strong enough to take care of you. She needs someone to care for her."

"I could have taken care of her," Chad said. "I told her I could."

When dinner was over, Roger said, "There's a good movie down at the drive-in. What say we pile in the car and go see it?"

Everyone was enthusiastic except Chad. "I don't feel much like going," he said. "I'll stay here."

"The movie's for you," Roger said. "I figured it might take your mind off things. If you don't want to go, we'll all stay home and play a game or something."

"Oh . . . no, I'll go." It felt odd to have even Roger worrying about him. "I'm awfully sorry I lost my temper," Chad added. "I'll pay for what I broke."

"No sweat. We'll replace the mirror at a garage sale and fix the chair."

"It's my temper. I get really mad sometimes."

"You think you have a temper? You should see Polly when she gets mad," Roger said. "Once she wrecked a living-room couch just because we had to take her puppy away."

"*You?*" Chad asked, unable to imagine quiet Polly in a rage.

Polly turned redder than her hair. "There was no reason that puppy couldn't be saved," she said tartly.

"The vet explained to you it was kinder to destroy him than to let him suffer," Roger said.

"It's never kind to destroy a living creature." Polly's eyes blazed fiercely. "You shouldn't give up on anything that's still got life in it."

123

"Polly might be a vet when she grows up," Pam said.

"I know," Chad said. Either a vet or a librarian she had told him.

The movie was funny in parts, and despite himself Chad did pay attention to it. He even laughed out loud once. Roger bought them all boxes of popcorn. The car was filled with the buttery aroma and the comforting closeness of all their bodies.

In the morning Chad woke up cold and thought of the cat, how it would be that last day when they drove off and left the cat behind. He cried some, just thinking about it. It was a rotten thing to teach someone to love you and then to leave him.

Chapter 13

One drizzling mean-tempered gray day followed another after Chad got the letter. The sky was continuously clotted with clouds. The cat never seemed to mind the weather, and rarely looked wet when Chad climbed the hill with a dish of milk or a can of the cat food Pam sometimes bought. The cat would be waiting for him, whiskers arched out, sitting proud and patient in the clearing under any sunbeams that had escaped the clouds. This morning it bounced over to Chad, tail up with the tip curved forward. Before Chad could set down the bowls of food, the cat began climbing up his jeans.

"Hey, what's with you, Cat?" Milk slopped over as Chad knelt with the cat hanging onto his belt. The cat nuzzled its head under Chad's arm, purring hoarsely. Chad held it and nuzzled back. "You're really full up with affection this morning, aren't you?" The cat rubbed and purred, then abruptly jumped off Chad and bent to eat its breakfast.

Chad watched, imagining the morning after the Sorenics and he had left the cottage empty. The cat would wait and wait in the clearing and then let out that absurd little wide-mouthed cry. It'd return the next day and the next and wait. Only Chad would never come back. Chad looked at the hole in his sneakers. No sense thinking about it. He couldn't do anything about the cat or himself. No sense thinking at all.

Chad rose and started off toward the marina. He had not seen the old man as often lately, not since Chester had learned his daughter wasn't coming after all. He'd go see how Chester was coming along. The cat appeared at his side to Chad's surprise. It walked sometimes a little ahead, to sniff at a dead fish mixed in with the seaweed, sometimes behind, but obviously keeping pace with Chad, who was tickled. The cat had never chosen to walk with him before. Chester was sitting on his box, a lumpish darkness in the light fog.

"Well," Chester said. "Both my friends come visiting this morning, I see." He threw a fish head toward the cat. "Here cat, saved this for you."

The cat, still full of breakfast, gave the fish head a disinterested sniff and then ignored it. It sat a few feet from Chester and Chad, completely at ease.

"You sure tamed him good," Chester said when Chad bent to pet the cat as it stretched up into his fingers, eyes shut in pleasure.

"We're leaving the Saturday after next," Chad said. "The cat'll have to get used to making it alone again."

"Life's tough, ain't it? And this winter's supposed to be a long one. Feller around here predicts early frost and a long, hard haul till spring."

The mournful sound of Chester's voice told Chad clearly how his friend was feeling. "Nothing ever comes out right," he said.

"You got problems, son?"

Chad didn't want to talk about his mother. "I don't like leaving the cat," he said.

"Well, no sense fretting over him. He survived one year alone, and he's smarter and tougher this year. Likely he'll make it through another."

"Yeah, sure, getting shot at by a psycho in the dump and freezing and hungry in a hard winter—great life."

"Summer comes round again most years."

"No," Chad said bitterly. "I don't know why nothing ever works out right—nothing." He clamped his jaw shut, dangerously close to whimpering.

Chester looked at him carefully. "What we gotta do, Chad, is learn to make do with the in-betweens."

"What's that?" Chad asked, sure they weren't anything he wanted.

"In-betweens is the good things, little things you don't think to ask for—like for me, you coming around to visit with me so regular this summer was a

127

good thing, a pleasure I never expected. Or like bright, sunny days when my legs don't ache. Or catching a run of blues and hooking a big one, or eating a piece of homemade blueberry pie my neighbor thought to share with me . . . in-betweens is surviving the winter and seeing spring come in one more time. There's always in-betweens to look for."

"So it doesn't matter that your daughter's not coming," Chad taunted, angry at the comfort that was no comfort at all to him.

"It matters. Course it matters. I'm just telling you how to cope, not that it's all rosy and easy."

The impulse to tell Chester about his mother's letter welled up in Chad and then sank. He didn't want to be told that the sun shone in the Boys' Home, too, if that was where he ended up.

"I don't much feel like fishing today," Chad said finally. "Maybe I'll come by tomorrow."

"Leaving so soon? . . . well, all right. I'll be looking for you tomorrow then." Chester looked as if he had more to say, but Chad didn't wait to hear it.

He started off the pier. The cat brushed his ankles, ready to follow him if he were going. Chad looked back at the old man. It struck him suddenly that he had started for the pier to give comfort, not to receive it. "Chester," he called impulsively, "I'm awfully sorry about your daughter. I really am."

"Maybe she'll come next year," Chester replied.

His smile lifted the corners of his beard and the knobs of his cheeks. "Maybe one of us will win some prize money. Or I could find a diamond ring inside a fish, maybe."

"That's a fairy tale."

"Well," the old man said, "nothing's wrong with fairy tales. Better than not believing in anything, ain't it?"

"Thought you were the one said there was no point hoping for anything."

"Did I say that? Not me." Chester waved him on with a smile.

Chester was just an old fool Chad thought as he ran back along the beach. He was nothing but a big old jerk, soft in the head, a mush brain—said one thing, said another. Chad didn't look to see if the cat was following him. In fact, he ran deliberately hard to get away. The cat would have to learn to do without him soon anyway.

Chapter 14

All through dinner Chad could feel something was stirring, something they all knew about and he didn't. It was the way everybody looked at each other and then away. But they all kept glancing at him.

"What's going on?" he asked finally.

"We're going to have a family conference after dinner," Roger said. "Don't anybody plan to go anywhere right away."

"Where's the big conference going to be, Dad?" Polly asked.

"How about right here at the kitchen table?" Pam said. "How about having it while we eat our ice cream?" With her soft smile and happy eyes, Chad knew it couldn't be anything bad, but they wouldn't want him around probably. He wasn't part of the family.

"Can I be excused?" he asked politely.

"You're in on the conference," Roger said. "In fact, you're the main subject of the conference."

Chad looked at Roger, trying to figure out what was up. Roger looked ready to burst, the way he got when he was excited or wanted to teach you something. He was like a kid trying to act grown up sometimes, but a decent kid with no meanness in him. They were all decent. Chad had been lucky this summer.

"What we want to talk about," Roger said, breaking into Chad's thoughts, "is your future."

"What about my future?"

"Well, we've been thinking—that is Pam and I, and Bob and Polly of course—we've been thinking that since you fit so well into our family, maybe you should become a part of it."

"I don't get what you mean." He did get it, but he wanted to be sure he was hearing right.

"What Roger is trying to say," Pam said, "is we'd like to adopt you if you're willing."

"Adopt me?"

"Of course, it would depend on what the caseworker says, and all the rigamarole of the agency. It would be a long process, but we didn't want to start it unless you thought you liked the idea," Pam continued.

Silence settled as Chad stared at each of the Sorenics in turn, seeing them with a new distinctness. They were nice people, a great family, but not *his* family. He didn't belong. He could never fit in.

"Well," Roger said, impatient as always. "What do you say, Chad?"

"Why would you want to adopt me? If you adopt me, the agency won't pay anything toward my upkeep anymore."

"We can't help it if we've got expensive tastes," Roger joked.

"I'm not all that smart either. I mean, I don't read books or anything."

"One bookworm in the family is enough."

"And I'm no athlete."

"We have one of those too."

"I have a rotten temper."

"We'll have to work on that."

"I haven't even been nice to you this summer," Chad said, after a pause.

Roger grinned. "Okay. So what do you say?"

"I don't know. I don't know what to think."

"Oh . . . well, give it time to sink in then. There's no rush." Roger sounded disappointed.

Chad felt strange. He didn't want to be adopted. He didn't want anybody to have rights over him. If he couldn't have his mother, he didn't want to be a family with anybody else. He'd rather be on his own. And it wasn't natural anyway. They were nice people but they were practically strangers. How could he be a family with them? He went up to the pine tree to brood.

The second morning that the cat didn't show for its breakfast, Chad started worrying. Had something happened to him? Chad went off to check with Mrs. Saugerty.

"I haven't seen him, not for weeks," Mrs. Saugerty said. "Haven't seen you either, Chad. Did you think I was mad at you?"

"I don't know."

"Well, I'm not."

"That's good."

"Will you be coming to work for me again soon?"

Chad hedged. "The summer's just about over," he said, and then he blurted out. "The Sorenics are thinking of adopting me though."

"You don't say! Well, isn't that nice. I'll bet you're glad about that."

"Maybe. Maybe I am. Anyway, maybe I'll be seeing you next summer."

"Maybe you will." Mrs. Saugerty smiled at him. "If I see your cat, I'll let you know."

Next day Chad and Polly walked down to the dock, but Chester was not there and neither was the cat. "I think something's happened to him," Chad said.

"Cats disappear for a while sometimes. It doesn't mean anything." Polly tried to reassure him.

"No," Chad replied. He had a foreboding that the cat's luck had run out. The more he thought about it, the more sure he was that his cat was dead.

On the third morning, Roger drove Chad and Bob to the dump. They unloaded the car and explored, each going in a different direction and calling and whistling for the cat. Nothing came in return but the squawking of the gulls and the smell of burning garbage.

"I'm gonna find that bulldozer guy and ask him," Chad announced.

"The guy with the gun? We'll all go," Roger said. "Get in the car." He drove them around the dirt roads separating the areas of the dump. The roads were like a maze going nowhere or circling back on themselves. Finally they spotted the yellow bulldozer, standing still. Jackson, the man with the big jaw, was leaning back against one of the wheels having a smoke.

"Hello there," Roger said walking up to Jackson, smiling in a slow, friendly manner. "Maybe you can help us. We've been looking for a black-and-white cat. He hangs around the dump a lot. Have you seen him recently?"

Jackson stared at Roger suspiciously and straightened up by easing his back up against the wheel. When he stood, he was looking down at Roger.

"A black-and-white cat—have you seen him?" Roger repeated.

Jackson shook his head slowly side from side.

"But he lives in the dump probably," Chad said. "You must've seen him."

"No," the man muttered.

"You took a shot at him once. We saw you," Chad said.

"All's I shoot is rats." Jackson set his mouth obstinately.

"About how long ago did you see him last?" Roger asked, still pleasant.

"I never seen no cat." The man looked tormented.

"Come on Chad, Bob. This is getting us nowhere." Roger put his hands on the boys' shoulders to draw them away.

"What a creepy guy," Bob said when they got back to the car.

Chad didn't say anything. He was imagining his cat lying on one of the piles of garbage with a bullet in him. But suppose he wasn't quite dead yet. Suppose he needed help.

"I'm going to stay here and look for the cat," Chad said with determination.

"No, you're not," Roger said, just as determined.

"I'll keep away from the guy, and I'll hitch a ride home from the main road."

"No," Roger said. "You're not staying here alone. It's not safe."

Chad tensed into himself, set to resist.

"Get into the car now, Chad."

Chad didn't budge. "I'm staying," he said and started off. Roger was not his father. No way did he have to listen to him, not when Chad knew the right thing was to stay.

"Chad, you know how big this place is. You couldn't find the cat even if he were here. Get in the car now. We'll circle round one more time—"

Chad didn't budge. What could Roger do about it? Hit him? Pick him up and throw him in the car?

"Polly and Pam are waiting for us," Roger said, still calm and reasonable. "We've been gone so long they're going to start worrying, especially since they know where we are. Who comes first, Chad, the cat or your family?"

"You're not my family."

"You mean, you've made your decision?"

"You're not my family *yet*," Chad said, and then quickly added, "Anyway the family isn't in trouble; the cat is."

"If he's alive," Roger said, "he's probably hiding out somewhere. Animals hole up if they get hurt. Or he might not even be here. He might be out courting a lady friend somewhere. Toms do that, and he'll drag in exhausted and make fools of us for worrying about him."

"You think he's hurt?"

Roger shrugged. "Could be. Could be he's picked up some sickness or he could have gotten hit by a car crossing the road or he could've gotten into a fight with another animal. There's no telling what could have happened to him."

"Or that guy could've shot him."

Roger grunted. "Suppose he did. How are you going to find him here?"

Chad looked around at the wasteland of bare dirt hills and garbage mounds. "I just want to look a while more," he said.

"I'll give you fifteen more minutes. Then we leave. Okay?"

Chad found himself nodding. Roger was fair. He had helped. Even now, Roger and Bob went off looking in directions parallel but apart from the one Chad took. They called and listened and called, and still the only answer was the seagulls' shrill cries and the sound of the bulldozer starting up.

In the car Roger said, "Don't feel so bad. He may come back before we leave and, if not, you could ask your fisherman friend to keep an eye out for him and drop you a postcard if he shows up."

"I feel like I've stolen his luck," Chad said.

"How did you figure that?"

"I get adopted and he gets dumped."

"I wouldn't have guessed from the way you've been acting that you considered yourself lucky—

that's what you're saying, isn't it?" Roger asked. "That you're lucky we want to adopt you?"

"Yeah . . . I know I'm lucky. It's just—"

"Just what?"

"Just I feel funny about it."

Roger nodded. Chad was glad Roger didn't ask him to explain what he meant. He couldn't have explained what he meant by "funny." Except that he still felt you had to be born into a family. You couldn't just move into one when you were half-grown, even a nice one like the Sorenics.

"Is it because you'd have to take me as your father?" Roger asked, keeping his eyes on the road ahead.

The question startled Chad. Didn't Roger know how much Chad thought of him? Awkwardly, Chad tried telling Roger how special he was. "I never had a father. You'd be the first."

Roger laughed. "That leaves me a clear field then."

Suddenly Chad felt good. He turned and grinned at Bob. "Hey buddy, how'd you like me for a brother?"

"I guess I can take it if you can." Bob was blushing, with a look in his eyes that convinced Chad that he had already said "yes" when the family asked him if he wanted Chad included in.

"Guess what!" Roger called when they walked into the cottage.

"You found the cat?" Pam answered.

"Not yet, but Chad's made his big decision. He's joining us!"

Pam clapped her hands and held her arms out, but Chad was looking at Polly, who was smiling the most beautiful, toothy smile at him. It was full of affection.

"My sister," Chad whispered. Joy shot up like a geyser inside him.

Finally he turned to Pam, still waiting there with her arms open. Then it hit him—what was wrong with getting adopted. He already had a mother. It didn't matter what a terrific lady Pam was; she couldn't be his mother, not when he already had one. His joy sank as fast as it had risen. He didn't want to hurt Pam's feelings, but he didn't want her expecting more than he could give either.

"I like you a lot, Pam," Chad faltered. "But the thing is, my mother—I mean I never had a father or a brother or a sister—but a *mother*—"

"I understand, Chad. Don't you worry. You and I will work out our own special relationship."

He couldn't believe anyone could be so understanding. In gratitude he went over and put his arms around Pam and hugged her. "Thanks," he said, and it didn't embarrass him at all that he was crying.

The next day Chad walked around in a happy haze that was only punctured every so often by the thought that the cat was still gone. It was funny, now that he felt so good, he could let himself hope that the cat would show up again. There was still a little time left. In the meantime he got a new thrill everytime he bumped into one of the family.

"Hi, Sis," he greeted Polly, who was reading in the living room.

"Oh, no!" she moaned, looking up from her book. "I just realized! *Two* brothers! As if one wasn't bad enough!" Then she pinched him for no reason and he had to chase her around the room until he caught her and made her say she was sorry.

In the afternoon he went up to the pine tree, so happy he felt capable of willing the cat to be there. But the cat didn't show.

Chapter 15

T hen time did run out. Everything except what they needed for the morning had been packed and was standing in the living room waiting to be loaded into the car. Bob and Chad and Polly began stuffing boxes and bags into the back of the station wagon after breakfast next morning while Pam nosed the vacuum cleaner around the already-cleaned cottage, worrying about corners that might have been missed.

It seemed to Chad they had more to take back now at the end of the summer than they had brought, even though they had not bought anything besides food. But they each had collections of shells and rocks, and there was the big driftwood root that Pam wanted to carry home for their backyard. The dried grasses and cattails that she and Polly planned to turn into flower arrangements needed space, too, and special handling.

When Roger saw the car, he complained, "Where do you expect me to fit my tools in?" He stood at the overstuffed back of the wagon with the tools in a packing case in his arms.

"On top?" Polly said.

"My *tools?*" Roger asked, and they all backed off sheepishly.

"There's still the leftover groceries to get in," Pam called from the doorway of the cottage. "Two bags of them on the kitchen table."

"I'll have to repack," Roger said. "Bob, Chad, help me unload the whole back."

Bob groaned. He and Chad began hefting out the boxes, bags, and loose, oddly shaped equipment they had shoved in any which way earlier in the morning. Spread on the ground, it looked as if two wagons wouldn't hold it all. "Okay now," Roger said. "Don't anybody put anything in. Just leave me alone to figure out how it should go."

Chad took one last walk up to the pine tree and sat down where he had sat the first time he had seen the cat. Like the cat, he himself had been a loner two months ago. Now he had a family to belong to, and only the cat was still unclaimed. He thought of the cat, tail up, sauntering down to the marina to visit Chester, sniffing through the wrack to see what the tide had brought in. It wasn't a bad life for a cat. A cat didn't need a family the way a kid did. Chad thought of the cat in the dump and wondered what kind of home he had there. Was it really a cozy berth for the winter or did the snow drift in; and what about when it rained for a week, and what about Jackson? Sure, Mrs. Saugerty had promised to put food out for the cat when Chad said he'd send her money for it, but still—Chad remembered the cat prancing over to him and piling in his lap, sure of a welcome.

"We're ready," Roger called.

Chad got up. One last time he called, "Here kitty, here kitty, kitty, kitty." And then the triangular head with the white exclamation mark alongside its nose poked through the bearberry leaves. Chad did a double take. The pink mouth stretched wide in an *Aarow* of greeting. The cat waited until Chad picked it up, then rubbed the back of its head on Chad's arm. A nearly healed scratch below one eye told of some recent battle, but otherwise the cat was sleek and looked as well fed as when Chad had served it its daily breakfast.

"Where *were* you all this time?" Chad asked as if the cat could answer.

"Told you not to worry," Roger said. "Cats do take off like that. It's their nature."

"Anyway, he came back in time."

"I think there's a box in the house you could put him in," Pam said.

"A box! I'm not putting this cat in any box."

"Well, you can't just hold him in your lap all the way home."

"Why not?"

"Try it and you'll see."

The family settled into the car. Chad carried the cat down, gently scratching behind its ears, while he eased in next to Polly. The cat tensed. Its eyes became round-black with alarm. Chad got a grip on it and reached to shut the door, but the cat clawed at Chad's arm and scrabbled loose. It jumped out and streaked back up the hill, instantly disappearing into the underbrush. Chad charged after it, calling, "Hey Cat, hey!" Then softly, over and over he begged, "Here, kitty. Here, kitty."

"You won't get him back for a while now—days maybe," Roger said.

Chad turned to see the family standing in a group back at the house, looking up at him with concern. The car waited for him too, doors open, loaded to the roof.

"What are we going to do now?" Bob asked.

Roger shrugged and looked unhappily at Chad. "What d'ya say?"

"If we catch him again, he'll *have* to go in a box," Pam said.

"We could drive over to the dump. He might be there," Polly offered.

Something clicked in Chad's mind. He saw a picture of the cat holed up somewhere watching them from its hiding place. It would watch until it thought it was safe to come out, until there was no chance they would enclose it in a car again, put it in a box, confine it. Cat was an independent. "Proud" was how Chester had put it once.

Chad thought of that morning when the caseworker had dumped him on the Sorenics just before they left for Cape Cod. He'd gotten a glimpse of their house then. It was near a busy shopping street, a narrow house packed in next to others like it without much yard or even many trees in which a cat could climb. Somehow Chad couldn't see the cat in that yard. Instead, he imagined it, tail up, sniffing at the tide's last leavings on the beach, prowling through the woods, independent, free.

"We're going to hit a lot of traffic if we don't get started soon," Roger said.

"Then let's go," Chad decided. He climbed back down the hill and got into the car without looking at anyone.

Uncertainly they followed him.

"But Chad, you can't just leave him here," Polly said.

"Sure I can. It's what he wants, Polly."

"But in the winter—"

"He'll survive. Mrs. Saugerty will feed him. He'll

be okay. You'll see. Next summer he'll be up there by the pine tree waiting for me."

"And if he's not?"

"He'll still be better off."

"You're sure?" Roger asked.

"Yeah," Chad said. "I'm sure." *He* couldn't make it on his own yet, but the cat could take care of himself. It wasn't right to take that away from him.

The car groaned into action, moving as if its bones ached like Chester's. Chad looked over his shoulder once, but he didn't see anything, not even a glimpse of the small triangular face peering through the green leaves after them. "Good luck, Cat," he whispered. "Say 'hi' to Chester for me when you see him."

About the Author

C.S. Adler was born in Rockaway Beach, New York, received her Bachelor's degree from Hunter College, and a Master's degree in Elementary Education from Russell Sage College in Troy, New York. She now lives in Schenectady, New York with her husband.

Ms. Adler wanted to be a writer from the time she was seven years old. In 1979 her first children's book, *The Magic of the Glits*, was published and won the Society of Children's Book Writers' Golden Kite Award. Since then, she has published three other children's books: *The Silver Coach, In Our House Scott Is My Brother*, and *Shelter on Blue Barns Road*. She explains how she feels about writing: "The best part about being a writer is that it keeps me from ever being bored. *Everything* is something to write about."

The Cat That Was Left Behind is C.S. Adler's first book for Clarion.